Angel IN THE Woods

Angel in the Woods

Copyright 2013 by Rachel Starr Thomson
Visit the author at www.rachelstarrthomson.com

Published by Little Dozen Press
Stevensville, Ontario, Canada
www.littledozen.com

Cover design by Mercy Hope
Copyright 2013

ISBN: 978-1-927658-19-2

Angel IN THE Woods

by Rachel Starr Thomson

TABLE OF CONTENTS

PART I

1. The Pixie..9

2. The Giant..13

3. The Darkwood..17

4. The Gaggle, the Poet, and Nora..21

5. The Manifold Secrets of Laundry..27

6. Evening in the Castle..31

7. Angel in the Dark..35

8. Intruder..41

9. The First Winter..45

10. Furs..51

11. In the Town..55

12. Lady Brawnlyn..61

13. The Widow's Commission..65

14. The Widow's Daughter..73

15. Independence..79

16. Brought Low..87

17. Illyrica..95

18. The Pixie Finds Help..103

19. A Long Night's Wait..111

20. The Angel Strikes a Bargain..123

21. Changes..133

22. Changes, Part 2..137

23. I Go Into Exile..141

24. Nora..147

PART II

25. Retrospect..153

26. A Deep Content..157

27. The Attack..161

28. Portent..169

29. We Withdraw...175

30. Collision...179

31. The Vigil...187

32. Genevieve...191

33. Before the Mob..197

34. Power in Papers...203

35. Home...209

36. Paradise Deepens...215

37. The Gentle Falling of Winter..219

38. All Things Well...221

PART 1

Chapter 1

THE PIXIE

NONE OF IT WOULD HAVE HAPPENED if they hadn't given the Pixie her wish and let her out of the castle for a day. She was about fifteen then, and terribly pretty in an elfin way. The lovely, impish look in her eyes had earned her nickname. There was a woman in there somewhere, set to emerge in a few years, but for the moment the Pixie was all girl. She appeared in the town and charmed the boots off the county folk within an hour or two. It was that charm, I suppose, which had gained her the unheard-of privilege of freedom. But alas, her personal appeal was quickly forgotten, buried under rumours that followed in her wake and left all the town buzzing. It is one of the glaring faults of humanity that it always finds gossip more interesting than truth.

Still, even our faults can sometimes lead to good. If it hadn't been for the Pixie's visit and the subsequent swirl of rumours, I might never have heard of the castle, or of the Giant in the woods who guarded it so fiercely.

I was a very young man in those days. I had left home three weeks earlier to make my way in the world, and had since discovered that one can sink to a level in life where a captivating aura lingers around words like "food" and "fireplace," while the shine of "adventure" begins to tarnish noticeably. I had been wrestling with this truth for two days. A small part of me was still stubbornly clinging to romantic hopes for my life while the other part of me was looking for a job.

Ah, but I looked, and there she was—the Pixie, all but dancing through the market with a look in her eyes that suggested the prosaic little street was a river of delights and she was drinking it in. She caught my eye for a moment, and something in her face sparked at the sight of me. And then the whispers began.

"She comes from the castle," said one.

"Must have escaped," said another.

"She trembles for her life," said an old, half-blind fellow. "Look how she peers every way. The Giant will be after her and bring trouble upon us all!"

The Pixie was hardly trembling, nor was she peering so much as she was taking everything in with a look of fascination and thinly-veiled mischief. But after all, there are few things more appealing to the romantic nature than a runaway maiden who is threatened by a giant. I listened to the rumours.

"Kidnapped as a baby, more than likely, just like the rest of them—poor, lovely things! They live in a castle out yonder, in the middle of a great forest. *He* keeps them there; he'll let no one near them!"

"Many's a young man has gone to their rescue, only to be torn to pieces by the Giant. A great, fierce beast is he. Big and black and strong as an ox."

"Every year in the harvest moon he roams the countryside and takes to himself a new one. One more house left destitute, and one more prisoner for the castle."

They were still talking when I stepped away from the rumour-mongers and began to walk through the market after the

Pixie. She had turned aside into a bookseller's stand, where she perused a little golden volume of oil paintings. She didn't seem to notice the whispering around her, but she noticed when I approached. She half-closed the book and looked up at me with a dazzling smile.

Any notion of true love and romance I held vanished as soon as she smiled at me. I had seen that look on female faces before: on the faces of my sister and adoring young cousins. The Pixie was a child—a captivating, bewitching child, but not one to be fallen in love with for a few years yet.

Somehow her youth made me feel more confident, and I imagined that I looked to her as mysterious as she looked to me. "They say you've run away," I said, as casually as if I'd asked about the book.

She laughed. "They would," she said. "Nora says they're all half-blind and very apt to jump to conclusions."

I decided not to comment on the wisdom of Nora and turn the conversation in another direction. I was disappointed that she hadn't run away. "Do you really live in a castle?"

"Oh yes," she said, her green eyes twinkling. "In the greatest, finest, dearest castle in the world."

The last adjective was disconcerting. I wondered if Nora had thought it up. I didn't have the opportunity to ask, for the Pixie lifted a slender arm and pointed off in a direction beyond the town. "It's that way," she said. "Down the road three miles, and then through the woods. At night it shines in the moonlight. You can hardly miss it."

"Shall I come and see you?" I asked.

"Oh yes," she said, laughing again. "If you're brave enough. You can join the Poet… only I think you're not as silly as he is."

RACHEL STARR THOMSON 11

Her eyes lit up. "You can help the children build the boat. Do you know anything about carpentry?"

"But what about the Giant?" I asked. If the rumours were true, my sparkling young friend was inviting me to my death without so much as a warning. I was already planning to take my chances, but it would only be decent of her to feel sorry for me. "The terrible Giant in the woods. They say he has killed many a man for daring to approach your home."

For an instant she looked puzzled, and then the lines of her forehead smoothed out and she gave the merriest laugh of all. Even as she laughed she began to move away from me. My feet seemed rooted to the spot.

"He is terrible enough if you cross him," she said. "But he's not exactly a giant. I think you must mean the Angel."

A minute later she was gone. She had, I think, moved quickly in an unexpected direction and been lost in the crowd. But to me in that moment it seemed she had been spirited away by some magical spell. She left me determined. I would seek out the castle and face whatever creature haunted the woods around it.

Chapter 2

———◆———

THE GIANT

"LAD," SAID THE VILLAGE BLACKSMITH the night I set out for the woods, "I think you a fool, though a brave one."

I lifted my cudgel—a good, heavy piece of wood, gift from the blacksmith himself—in a salute and smiled broadly. The housewife's stew was still warm in my belly, and it filled me with courage. The summer night air was warm and breezy, not in the least oppressive. I couldn't have been afraid, there in the village street below the wainwright's door—not if I had tried.

I remained confident even after I left the borders of the town and strode down the road in the moonlight. Not until the forest loomed up before me did I begin to quail, but I saw a path and took it. The woods were alive in the darkness. Creatures stirred beyond my vision. The trees grew taller and blacker and reached down with long branches. The forest seemed to be closing in around me. I gripped my cudgel all the tighter. So much did I concentrate on putting one foot in front of another that I forgot to take heed to the path, and before long I realized that I was lost.

Then I saw it. A distant glow through the trees. For a moment I thought the sun was rising. I must have been lost in the woods far longer than I had imagined—morning already! But no, I was mistaken. Now it seemed to me that I saw the light of a great pearl; or perhaps the moon had come to Earth. The moon… yes, now I remembered. The Pixie had told me that the castle shone in the moonlight. It was the castle walls, then, that glimmered before me. It could not be much farther.

I stepped forward with renewed vigour. In that instant a great wooden spear cut through the air just in front of me and lodged in the ground; its head buried deep and its thick oaken length trembling. I whirled around, brandishing my cudgel in the air.

I heard his voice—deep, fearsome, unearthly voice—before I saw him.

"Why have you come here?" he demanded.

I gathered my courage and answered, though my voice trembled. "I have come to seek the Giant in the darkwood," I said.

Still he remained in the shadow of the trees, his form much like theirs—huge and solid, round like an oak. "To what purpose?" he asked, his voice so low it seemed to make the branches shake.

"To see for myself whether he be angel or demon," I answered.

The Giant took a step nearer to me, and I saw him more clearly. He was a man, a great man, who dwarfed me as a mountain dwarfs a hill. His clothes were dark. I could not tell from them whether he was rich or poor. A black beard covered most of his face. I could see his eyes in the darkness: large eyes, dark and glowering.

"An angel?" the Giant rumbled. "And who, in your hearing, called me that?"

"A girl," I said. I regained some confidence, and my voice did not shake so much now. "A girl in the village marketplace, not three days ago."

The Giant began to move again. Tree branches cleared back from him as though they were blown by a strong wind. It was hard to follow him in the shadows, but he seemed to be circling me; assessing me.

"And if I be a demon?" the Giant asked. "What will you do?"

"I will seek to slay you," I answered him, "and free the innocents you hold captive."

"With a stick?" the Giant asked.

My eyes flickered away from the shadows, down to my cudgel. I had been gripping it so hard that my fingers ached.

"I will try," I said.

For a moment the Giant said nothing, and I had the uncomfortable feeling that he was laughing at me. Then his voice boomed out again.

"And if I be an Angel?"

"Then," I stammered, "then... I would hope to learn from you."

His tone grew quieter. Sterner. "Are you lovesick? Are you here for the sake of the girl in the marketplace?"

"She is very young," I said.

"You are not so much older," he answered.

"I would help her, if she needs help," I said. "But I have no other motive."

"Then stay," he said. "Stay in the woods. Do not come one step nearer to the castle, on pain of your life. Whatever comes your way in the night, do not allow yourself to be moved. I will send for you in the morning. *If* you are still here, we shall talk again."

He did not wait for me to answer. More suddenly than any creature his size should be able to move, he was gone. I was left alone in the woods.

Chapter 3

———◈———

THE DARKWOOD

T HE GIANT HAD NOT BEEN GONE ten minutes when a shadow fell across the moon. The wood was plunged into darkness so deep that it ceased to be mere darkness. It became a force, heavy and oppressive. The glow of the white castle walls disappeared entirely.

Behind me, something stirred.

I whirled around. Another sound—overhead now, snapping twigs and rustling in the dying leaves. My heart was in my throat as I spun again, trying to find the threat. A flap of wings—it flew away. A night bird. Nothing more. I stood staring up at the place where it had been, but still I could see nothing.

The fingers of fear began to curl around the back of my neck. Was something there? Moving? Waiting? I couldn't see. The darkness was a fiend meant to keep me blind. This was no test of my resolve—it was a trap.

I saw something in the trees. Massive and silent. I saw the sword in his hand. The Giant himself had come to strike me down in the terrible darkness. With a yell, I leapt at him, swinging the cudgel with all my might. I would take him down at the knees, as I was not tall enough to deal a blow to his head.

The cudgel cracked in my hands. The noise of it resounded in the stillness. The sound of it echoed in my heart, along with the sound of my own voice, crying out in rage, in terror, in what I hoped was courage.

But there was nothing there. I had attacked a tree.

I couldn't even laugh at myself. I backed away slowly from the trees, back into the clearing where the Giant had left me alone… but not alone. There were a thousand frights and specters in the woods. I knew I had made a fool of myself, but I was not humble enough to be freed by the knowledge. Shame only made my fear sharper.

Against every natural inclination, I forced myself to stay where I was. Slowly, I lowered myself to the ground, my back against a tree trunk I could not even see. I sat there, alone in the darkness, curled up with the splintered cudgel still held tightly in my hands. The Giant had left me only one command: stay where I was till morning. I meant to succeed.

I do not know how long I remained frozen there, every sound and movement putting me more on edge. After a time some small measure of light began to come back. The tangle of branches and leaves above me was outlined against the moon. Slowly I stretched out my legs again, laid the cudgel down by my side, and relaxed. My eyelids began to grow heavy.

I was nearly asleep when I saw a soft light coming toward me.

The light moved gracefully through the trees. As it came nearer I made out the form of a young woman in the center of it: lovely, carrying a lantern that made her golden hair and white dress glow. My heart pounded with new longing when I saw her. I struggled to my feet, shaking off the sleep that had settled over me.

She smiled as I stood, and held out her hand. "Come with me," she said. Her tone was half command, half question.

"I will come," I told her. The cudgel lay forgotten at my feet. I was bewitched.

I took a step toward her—and a voice rose up deep inside me and demanded to know where I was going.

I asked her the same question.

She turned and smiled again, a gentle, sweet smile. "To the castle, where my sisters and I are mistresses," she said. "You must come and sleep in safety and comfort."

My feet seemed suddenly rooted to the spot.

"I cannot follow you," I said. "I will not move a step closer to the castle till morning."

The look in her eyes was reproving as she regarded me. "You have already passed the test," she told me. "You have withstood the darkness so completely that fear has fled, and you are free to come to our home."

I shook my head, aware that I looked dirty and childish. "I will not," I said.

Her eyes filled with sorrow. I could hardly bear to look at her. Had I allowed myself to gaze on her, I would have lost all resolve; for how could I resist? But I cast my eyes down and refused to look up again.

"Please," she said, her voice almost a whisper. "Come and help us."

Once more I shook my head. A moment later the light was gone. I looked up in surprise. The young woman had disappeared.

Hours or minutes or years later, I found myself lying on the ground, covered in dew and blinking in the light of the rising sun. I was still in the clearing where the Giant had left me.

I never knew how much of that night in the darkwood was real, and how much I had dreamed. I did not have time to speculate, for as I pushed myself up onto my knees in the morning light, I saw a small procession coming toward me from the castle.

Chapter 4

THE GAGGLE, THE POET, AND NORA

I COULDN'T IMMEDIATELY TELL, upon seeing the procession, just what composed it. It was overwhelmingly pastel, energetic, and what is more, it was giggling. I do not just mean that the various parts of the procession were giggling. No, laughter to them was something done as a body. They had to come down a bit of a hill to reach me, and so I saw that they were smaller than I had first thought them. The procession was, in fact, made up of little girls. They wore pretty frocks, clean and starched, with white stockings and beautiful little buckled shoes, and their hair was long and tied back with ribbons. One of them, a very small child with yellow curls and serious eyes, held a long-suffering white goose in her arms. I was almost afraid she was going to offer it to me, but she did not. She just stood and looked at me while the others began their examination.

A trio of girls poked and pulled at one of my arms, and one grabbed my hand and looked it over. "He'll do!" she said. "He's made boats before, I'm sure!"

One dark-curled child beckoned to me with her finger. I leaned over so that I might look her in her blue eyes. "Have you built boats?" she asked.

"I haven't," I confessed. "But I have built bookcases."

"We don't need those," she told me, sadness coming over her face.

"I can learn to build boats," I told her, suddenly afraid lest the girls should find fault with me. "Indeed, I can learn very fast."

The child before me smiled. Her face was radiant when she did. "I'm Izzy," she told me.

"Certainly not," I rejoined. "You must be Isabelle."

She smiled even more. "Only the Poet calls me that."

"You don't mind if I do?" I asked.

She shook her head, dark curls bouncing around her shoulders. "I think it's a beautiful name," she said.

(Off to one side, the child with the goose was looking into the woods with her head cocked slightly. "Angel?" she said, but there was no answer.)

A younger child, probably four or five, tugged at Isabelle's hand. "Izzy, Izzy," she said. "Let's go back! Nora said not to be long. And if we help with the laundry, we can build the boat."

Accordingly, they started back at once, pulling, pushing, and sweeping me along with them. As we made our way up the hill, the Castle appeared before me in all its glory.

It was a great house, and very old, built of massive grey stones. In places it was nearly overgrown, but here, as we headed across the front lawn, everything was well-kept and beautiful. We passed beds full of flowers and stately old trees that made shady places especially for children to take shelter in on hot days. The front doors, I realized, were standing open, but the room beyond was in shadow. Before the doors, a great mess of contraptions and wash basins and lines had been set out, and females of various young ages were hard at work washing linens and hanging them up to dry. Multitudinous sheets already waved gently in the breeze, like sails over a sea of green grass. In the center of all the commotion, a young woman was bent over a washtub. She looked up as we approached and took everything in with one sweep of her eyes. I recognized the look on her face. It was no-nonsense, dreadfully grown-up, and more importantly to me, distinctly unwelcoming.

I did not have time to tangle with the owner of the imposing face, for a male voice suddenly called across the lawn, startling me. I turned and saw a slender man beckoning to me from behind a tree.

"Ho, you there!" he called. "Come and speak with me, good sir!"

There could be no doubt that he was addressing me. I was the only "sir" in the immediate area. I looked around to seek permission, but none of the gaggle protested. Half of them had already skipped away to other parts of the lawn, and some were playing hide-and-seek behind the laundry. The imposing face might have had something to say about it, but I quavered slightly at meeting her just then, so I made my way across the lawn to the willow where the man waited.

He was, as I said, a slender fellow. I'd no doubt I could have easily pounded him into the ground. My feeling of superiority deepened as he was slightly flushed and obviously uncomfortable with meeting me, even if he had initiated the meeting. He wore fine clothes, with billowy sleeves and a golden belt, and a small lute hung from his shoulder.

"Look here," he said. "Did the Angel truly tell you you could stay here?"

"He did," I said, though I wasn't at all sure what the Angel had told me I could do.

RACHEL STARR THOMSON 23

"Oh dear," the man said. "Do you mean to tell me that you… that you actually saw him?"

"Well, yes," I answered. "It was dark, but I saw him. Have you never seen him?"

He shook his head mournfully. "Not in all the months I've been here. He watches me, but has never given me the honour of seeing him." He looked up at me. I was rather taller than he was, and I felt that my shoulders were very broad. "Was he very fearsome?" he asked.

I lowered my voice. "Indeed," I said. "He would terrify a lesser man."

The man nodded again. Then he seemed to gather up his courage. He stood up to his full height and looked me in the eye. "Look here," he said, "I don't know why you've come, but if you're after Illyrica, I shall fight you for her."

I shook my head, trying not to laugh. "I am not, as you say, 'after' anyone."

The man heaved a sigh. "Three passages of the moon I have been here this time—three months. I sing and I play—I woo her with all the gifts given me, with my pen itself, and with what does she reward me? A smile here, a token there… ah, but I would die for her smile."

He was a ridiculous little man, and suddenly I knew he was the one the Pixie had called "the Poet." But for all his woe and billowy sleeves, I thought I saw sincerity and a true heart in him. I placed my hand on his shoulder. "Be a man of honour," I told him, "and I shall put in a word for you with Illyrica."

He brightened immediately. "Oh, I say," he said. "That's very kind of you."

Someone tugged on my hand. I looked down to see a small member of the gaggle. "Come," she told me. "You must come and see Nora."

I nodded my good-bye to the Poet, who seemed very much bettered by my promise to him, and followed the child back across the lawn where the laundry was still being done. This time the young woman was not bent over her tub. She was standing, very straight and tall and slender, and her arms were folded. She was looking right at me.

"I suppose you're waiting for a welcome," she said. The words were stern, but there was some good humour in them. "Don't expect anything too grand. This may be a castle, but you'll not be a lord in it."

I recognized the tone at once. This was the Nora the Pixie had spoken of, who made condescending comments about townspeople.

As if to confirm my guess, a whirlwind of colour and loveliness appeared from behind a nearby sheet, and the Pixie let out a whoop of delight. "It's you!" she said. "I knew it would be you. Nora, the boy from the market has come. Boy, this is Nora. She's all of our mother, and sister, and best friend in the world."

Nora's eyes softened considerably when the Pixie appeared. She even managed a smile. The smile was not for me. I couldn't imagine that she'd ever be <i>my</i> best friend, or sister or mother either. But I stepped forward, bowed, and said, "My name…"

The Pixie cut me off. "None of that," she said. "No one brings outside names here. I name you Sparrowhawk, because you're strong and you have very interesting eyes, and you're looking for something."

Nora's eyes met mine in that moment. There was a question in them. A challenge. Almost a threat. She wanted to know what I was looking for. I cleared my throat, intending to find words to answer her question. To tell her that I had come in search of adventure, that I was a boy trying to make the journey to manhood, and that I thought I could make a name for myself here somehow. But the intensity of her look stole my ability to speak. I felt suddenly like a marauding weasel looking into the eyes of a she-wolf whose children I had threatened to disturb.

She looked away, hefted a pile of laundry in her arms, and thrust it at me. "Fold these," she said.

So I did.

Chapter 5

THE MANIFOLD SECRETS OF LAUNDRY

THERE ARE FEW THINGS more damaging to a young man's ego than to be told that he cannot fold a sheet properly to save his life. Nora told me so, without care for my pride, as she shook out the sheets I had just finished and refolded them, moving with an expert grace and speed that put me to shame. The Pixie laughed gaily when she heard it, also without regard to my feelings, and took my arm.

"Let him come with me, Nora," she said. "He can help me hang the curtains."

Following the Pixie into the castle with my arms full to the bursting with curtains, I found it in me to wonder how I, the wandering hero, came to be doing housework. The open doors led into a shallow room with a high ceiling and green rugs, from which various other doors concealed passages that led into other parts of the great stone house. I followed the Pixie through a door to the left, up a flight of stone steps along which open windows let in the breezy glory of the morning. I staggered slightly under my load but was careful not to let her see it, and all the while questions ran up and down staircases of their own in my head.

A girl of about twelve passed us on the steps, greeting the Pixie and favouring me with a stare. A few minutes later another skipped by, singing to herself. (I was quickly discovering just how many steps a castle can harbour, and how blithely a Pixie can charge up them without a thought for the weight of curtains—but I did not complain.) The appearance of the girls quickened my questions. Who were they? Where had they all come from? From the rumours of the townspeople I had expected to find the lot of them imprisoned against their wills and imperiled by some evil force, but from what I had seen they were menaced by nothing more frightening than Nora and her laundry tubs. *Peril enough*, I thought to myself as the Pixie called back that it was "just a little farther." Yet there was still that terrifying figure in the woods. The memory of the Giant fell over me like a shadow. The stairs ended. The Pixie pushed a pair of doors open, and I found myself standing in a magnificent library with high, curtainless windows through which the sun was streaming gloriously.

The Pixie soon had me climbing a ladder beside the windows, dragging a heavy length of purple cloth up to the top rungs, where I balanced precariously while she ran nimbly up another ladder and fiddled with draping the curtains every which way. My perch afforded me a good look out the window. The library looked down on more lawns, rolling away from the castle in beautiful green patches criss-crossed with rose bushes and hedging. Beyond that the woods rose, menacing and dark.

Once more I felt that a shadow had fallen over me. The woods surrounded the castle completely, and somewhere in their dark fastness the Giant waited, coming upon unsuspecting travelers in the night. I didn't know why he had let me through, but I was struck by how otherworldly this place was—how isolated, how full of mystery. I cast a sidelong glance at the Pixie, her face flushed and lovely as she leaned over the window, the sunlight catching in her hair and the warm colours of books framing her.

She *was* a prisoner here. They all were, in some way I couldn't understand.

A movement on the lawn caught my eye. It was the Poet, strolling along with his lute in his arms, strumming to himself. I gestured at him.

"Doesn't he help with the laundry?" I asked.

"The Poet?" the Pixie said. "Oh, no."

I managed a smile as the Pixie pulled a length of cloth from my hand, unsettling my balance in a way I didn't like. "Seems a bit unfair," I said.

"Not at all," she answered with a twinkle in her eye. "The Poet is a genius. He… writes."

She had finished with her end of the curtains, so she issued orders for my corner and I followed them. As I descended the ladder, I took in the long rows of musty old books and the paintings that hung here and there among them. The library had the feel of a room well-used and well-loved, but very old.

"Whose house is this?" I asked.

The Pixie gave me a strange look. "Ours," she answered.

"It must have belonged to a very old family," I said. "Some of these books look generations in age."

"I suppose so," the Pixie said.

I caught her eyes suddenly. "Where did you come from?" I demanded. My stomach twisted in a peculiar fashion as I asked it.

The Pixie looked at me for a long moment. I thought she seemed worried—as though we shouldn't be talking about such things. "I don't know," she told me at last.

"Well, don't you want to know?" I asked.

I had asked the wrong question. The Pixie turned on her heel and left the room. I remained, with an armload of curtains at my feet and a heart wracked by guilt. I had broken the Pixie's merry exterior, and somehow I felt that I had done something terribly wrong.

Minutes later, one of the library doors opened and the Pixie reentered. Her expression was solemn, but she was not angry with me. She approached me slowly, almost reverently, holding a bit of cloth in her hand. She stopped a few feet away and held it out to me, the sun's rays picking up bright strands of thread and making them shine.

I took it hesitantly. She was waiting, so I looked away from her face and down at the cloth in my hand. It was silk, its edges ragged as if it had been torn from a larger piece. Embroidered in delicate green and purple thread were the letters *R.S. F.*

"This is all I have from my old life," the Pixie said. "I can remember nothing. So you tell me. Where did I come from?"

I wanted to answer her, but there was nothing I could say. She took the scrap of cloth back and laughed at me. "You look as though I'd just handed you a death warrant," she said.

"Well…" I answered, "well, doesn't it make you sad?"

The Pixie's eyes were twinkling again. "No," she said. "Not especially. But it gives me an air of mystery, which I like. And it's more than most of the girls have. Come, Sparrowhawk. There are other windows to curtain. And many more steps to climb."

I followed her out of the library with my arms full of drapery, glad that the conversation, for now at least, was over.

Chapter 6

——◆——

EVENING IN THE CASTLE

I FOLLOWED THE PIXIE AROUND for nearly two and a half hours, hanging curtains in a vast multitude of rooms. By the end of it my arms and back ached and I was beginning to feel more and more likely to fall off a ladder in a moment of exhaustion and die. My eyes were tired from the sun's pouring into them all morning. At home I had never given thought to the work our housekeepers did. I would have pooh-poohed the very idea that they might like a young man's help. Now I was beginning to feel sorry for them.

Despite her prosaic occupation, the Pixie grew more mysterious to me by the minute. The scrap of cloth with its initials fascinated and haunted me. She might be royalty, kidnapped from her cradle so some despot could have her throne and left here to live in obscurity forever under the Giant's dreadful eye. Or perhaps her mother had been a fugitive from a foreign land, and had given the Pixie the scrap of cloth to somehow lead her back home—or else the Giant had simply taken her from some happy cottage somewhere. The possibilities were endless, and the Pixie, with her radiant beauty and laughing eyes, seemed to fit every one perfectly.

And then there were the others: all the others. They seemed to come from every nook and cranny in the castle, their numbers growing all the time: forty or more of them, with Nora the oldest and unchallenged leader; the Pixie their muse; and Illyrica, whom I nearly knocked over by turning around quickly without realizing she was behind me, their pale and silent ghost. The three were the oldest of the Giant's charges, and the little girls adored each of them in their own way.

The sun began at last to set behind the great trees. It cast rays of fairy light over the lawns and gardens. I had been huddled with the gaggle for some hours around a heap of lumber near a small creek that ran behind the house, trying to make sense of the piles of lumber and half-attempts at building which they called a boat. With the setting of the sun they began to tug at my hands, leading me out from the deep green shadows of willow and water back toward the house, whose white stone walls glowed with the pinks and purples of the sky, deepening in a velvet twilight.

We passed through the wooden doors, and music greeted my ears: the soft plucking of a lute, a serene, welcoming song that held in its notes the good-hearted dying of the day. I expected to see the Poet, but he was nowhere in sight. Rather, the Pixie was seated on a wooden bench in the flagstone entryway, the Poet's lute cradled in her arms, smiling and greeting each of the children in turn with her eyes. She turned her eyes on me as well, but it was not with the same look of welcome. For once her look was inscrutable.

The doors to a large, soft room were thrown open, and into it the children pulled me. It was soft, I say, because it was furnished with hundreds of cushions and curtains, and deep rugs adorned the floor. Flames danced merrily in fireplaces at each end of the room, and the occupants of the house were already gathering around them; sitting in little circles, laughing and talking. At one end Illyrica sat with two little girls in her lap and one hanging around her neck, a look of contentment on her face. The girls chattered merrily to her, but not a word did she answer. Illyrica never did, for she was mute. She was a pale, ethereal beauty, with white-blonde curls that she tied at the nape of her neck and blue eyes that spoke more eloquently than voice ever could—but only rarely did they say anything. Illyrica kept her own counsel, even with her eyes. The one flaw in her beauty was a scar across her throat. Though no one ever told me so, I supposed it to be the cause of her silence.

Nora sat cross-legged at the other end of the room, surrounded by little girl-children who lay in every possible position on the cushions all round. A thick golden book lay open in her lap, and she was reading from it. Her voice was quiet yet commanding, and her audience was riveted. She looked a very different figure here than she had standing marshall over the laundry pots. Her face was rosy from the day's work, and her eyes shone with deep delight—whether in the children or in the story, I could not tell.

Isabelle and the others who had brought me in let go of my hands and rushed to join their comrades around Nora. She looked up when they joined her. Something fell over her face when she saw me, and her voice faltered, but a moment later her shoulders were square and resolute and I was ignored as she continued to read. I was saved from awkwardness when the Pixie appeared behind me, the lute forgotten, and clapped her hands. The whole room surged to their feet at once, and the soft room was abandoned for the dining hall.

Fresh bread graced the supper table, with cherries from a nearby orchard and a great pot of hot chocolate. I filled up on it well enough. I might have wished for a leg of meat or a tankard of ale, but either would have seemed madly out of place in the great white house. When dinner had ended the whole tribe returned to the soft room. I followed them, to find that an enormous wooden chair had been brought out of hiding and placed in the center of the room. The children had arranged themselves all around it. The Giant sat there in the midst of them. Illyrica rested on the floor on one side of him with her head on his knee, and the Pixie sat on the other side. Nora stood behind the Giant with her eyes full.

I had not seen the Giant in the light before. I saw now that he was a very great man in stature, but only a man. His thick hair and beard, once coal black, were beginning to grey. He wore dark peasant clothes, and his massive hands were worn and wrinkled. He looked up and saw me. His eyes seemed to declare his pride in his little kingdom, and yet I thought I saw tears in them. The next instant he blinked, and the illusion was gone.

"Will you not stay with us this time, Angel?" the Pixie asked. Every child in the room leaned forward to catch his answer, but he shook his great shaggy head and looked at me again.

"No," he said in a deep, gruff voice. "No, my girls, I have only come for that one there."

He pointed a finger at me. Every head turned my way.

Every head but Nora's. Her eyes were resolutely on the floor, and she would not look at me.

Chapter 7

————◆————

ANGEL IN THE DARK

I LEFT THE CASTLE THAT NIGHT and went with the Giant deep into the woods. I did not know, when I turned my head to see the white stones disappearing behind the trees, that I would not enter the castle again for three months; nor would I speak to its inhabitants in all of that time.

I followed the Giant through the woods until we reached a moonlit clearing. He knew it intimately, for he stretched out his hand and brought forth a staff that had been leaning against a tree, invisible in the night. He tossed it to me. I caught it, surprised.

"You threatened me once with a stick," he said. "So. Fight."

I saw that he had another staff in his hands, held at ready. I tightened my grip on the staff, feeling its weight in my hand, watching the Giant. I knew that my smaller size could be a boon, for I had agility that the Giant did not have—and I was by far the younger man, and the quicker. I thought I saw my chance. I moved in to strike him. In the next instant I lay flat on my back, gasping for breath.

"On your feet," the Giant commanded. "Again."

I struggled to my feet, letting the sting of pain and pride give me strength. I crouched lower this time, circled him more warily.

Again I moved; again he bested me with such speed that I had no time to see it coming.

We sparred that night until my body ran with sweat. Over and over he defeated me, until my limbs and back ached. I wondered if he had not brought me here to kill me after all—if he was not the villain I had first imagined him to be. Yet he did not seem interested in killing me. After an hour, when I once more lay on the ground with my chest heaving and my limbs crying out in protest, the Giant reached down his hand.

"Will you let me help you up, boy?" the Giant asked.

"I am not a boy," I gasped.

"No," the Giant said. "Only a mule is so stubborn that he will not be helped. Stand, then."

I struggled to my feet. The world reeled around me as I did. I tried desperately to stay standing. The Giant's gruff voice broke through the haze of my mind. I did not hear everything he said, but the word "drink" struck my ear.

"Yes," I gasped. In a moment the rough skin of a drinking horn was thrust into my hand. I poured the cool water down my throat as greedily as any ill-trained child. But oh, my whole body thrilled to it!

The Giant stood and watched me. When I had finished, the world had stopped spinning quite so dizzily.

"Are you in pain, boy?" he asked.

"No," I lied.

The Giant grunted. He thrust something into my hand—a spear. I could see its tip glinting in the moonlight.

"You'll be hungry," he said. "Feed yourself."

He meant that I should hunt—in the middle of the night! I nearly laughed at the idea. "It is dark," I said.

Somewhere in the trees, an owl hooted. "All the wisest hunt at night," the Giant answered.

"You misunderstand me," I said. "I cannot hunt now; I cannot see."

"Only a fool trusts to his eyes," the Giant said. "You remember that. The eyes can only show you the appearance of things. You will never understand anything until you learn to look past appearances."

I was sure he was not really speaking of hunting, but his true meaning I could not get at. Not then.

I caught nothing that night, and the Giant did not share his catch with me. He might have, if my pride had not been stronger than my stomach. I rebuffed any compassionate gift he might have been tempted to bestow. Nor did I catch anything the next night, or for many nights thereafter. Thankfully, the Giant taught me the art of setting and checking traps; else I should have eaten nothing but berries and bark for months—and even these, I had to find myself. The Giant taught me always in the dark. My eyes grew more adept at seeing in shadow. I learned to recognize good food from bad by the smell and feel of it, to find my way by the bare outlines of branches and the patterns in what seemed like hopeless tangles of roots and moss, by the occasional glimpse of moon and stars. At long last I learned to throw a spear in the darkness and have it find its mark, and then I ate meat and was more glad of it than I could say. I thought my heart would swell to bursting as I sat by the fire and roasted that creature. I had done it. I had learned.

As my lessons lasted all through the night, I made myself a den under the roots of an ancient oak, where I slept in the earth's darkness late into every morning. In the afternoon I would emerge, to spend my day as I liked. In the lazy days of summer I fished in the creeks that ran through the woods, and I roamed the forest paths for a few hours each afternoon, trying to match up the world I knew in darkness with the world I saw in light. I began after a while to understand the Giant's words, or to think that I did. The world was deeper in the night. In the day I could convince myself that I saw everything there was to see, but darkness forced me to know the woods in greater measure.

I came to know the darkwood as though it was an extension of myself. To move as silently as a wolf in the trees. To pay attention to every sound and smell and movement. But as well as I knew the woods, the Giant knew them far better. Where he went in the day I did not know. His manner did not welcome questions. He came to me after dark every night, and we hunted together, or sparred as we had the first night, though he was gentler with me now. Toward dawn we would light a fire and sit by it, eating whatever we had caught that day. Often I saw by the light of the fire that there was blood beneath his fingernails and in the deep cracks of his hands, but I never asked about it. I grew to respect the Giant as I had never respected any man. He was wise in the way of the woods as no man I had ever imagined. His strength was enormous, yet he was quiet and gentle in it. His speech was gruff, yet there was more in what he said than I could easily understand.

Summer drew near its close, and the night air began to take an edge to itself. The Giant handed me a cloak of furs one night. I looked at him quizzically.

"It is yours," he said.

"I did not work for it," I said. "You have never given me anything I did not work for."

The Giant looked at me for a long moment over the light of the bonfire. "A man must always use his hands in honest work when he has a need," he said at last. "But he must also humble himself. If you cannot accept a gift from a friend, then you are still a fool."

I did not say another word about it. That night I slept warmly, couched in my den with the thick fur all around me.

It was not long after that the Giant came to me earlier than usual, when the sun was only halfway down its descent. His staff was in his hands. With his head he gestured toward mine.

"Take it up, boy," he said. "Show me what you have learned."

I took up the staff, my heart pounding with strange eagerness. Never once had I beaten the Giant since that first night in the woods, but I had grown in strength and agility. The twilight played tricks with my eyes, but I knew it did the same to him. We circled each other warily. I moved in. The clearing echoed with the sound as wooden staff hit wooden staff. He struck, and I countered; I swung for him, and he jumped back. An instant later his staff swung into my back, and I fell to the ground, the wind knocked out of me. I struggled to breathe as I pushed myself up on the palms of my hands.

"What hurts, boy?" the Giant said.

I looked up at him, fire in my eyes. "I think you have bent my spine," I told him.

He shook his head. To my surprise there was sorrow in his expression. "Better that your pride should hurt," he said. "Let it hurt, boy; let it break. Pride is your greatest enemy."

I saw my chance. The Giant was not paying attention as he usually did. I leapt to my feet, catching up my staff as I did so, and brought it sharply against the back of his knees. I stood straight even as he hit the ground. He looked up at me and grimaced. I could only look down at him, my hands gripping the staff, my chest heaving as I fought to regain control of my breath. I had imagined beating him a thousand times, but I felt no triumph now.

The Giant held out his hand. "Help me to my feet, boy," he said. It was a moment before his words registered, and then I scrambled to catch hold of his hand and help him up.

On his feet again, the Giant laid his hand on my shoulder. I looked up at him, stilled by the gentleness in his eyes. "You have learned a great deal," he said.

"I…" I stammered, trying to find my tongue. The Giant had not spoken so directly to me since I had come to the woods with him, and I was suddenly overwhelmed by a feeling of indebtedness. "I thank you, Angel."

His hand tightened on my shoulder, and he smiled.

And then the moment was broken. He looked away suddenly, deep lines furrowing his brow. I started to ask him what was wrong, but he held a finger to his lips.

Faster and more silently than any man his size should have been able to move, he plunged into the forest. I followed him. He had not told me that I could not come, and I wanted to know what was happening. As I moved down the well-known paths in the footsteps of the Angel of the Woods, a chill came over me. Something was wrong. I could feel it in the air; sense it in the silence of the night-creatures.

There was an intruder in our world.

Chapter 8

※◆◆※

INTRUDER

A BRIGHT MOON SHONE OVERHEAD, illuminating silver pockets of darkness as we moved through the wood. We were on high ground, and the trees were sparser than in most places, but I did not fear that anyone would see us coming. The Giant wore dark clothes as he always did, and I had long since traded my traveler's garb for furred buckskin. I was as grey and drab as an aging deer; and if I did not move with his grace, I had at least learned the deer's trick of silence.

The Giant stopped abruptly at the edge of a low ridge overlooking a wide path. It was the road I had used when I first entered the wood, the remnant of what had once been a well-traveled drive. The forest had encroached much upon it, but it was still clearly distinguishable as a man-made path, and it led straight to the castle.

Something was coming down it, something too clumsy and careless to belong to the woods, though quiet enough for a man. I peered down into the gloom of the road, and then I saw him—a small, hunched man, who moved with many a furtive look in every direction, and clutched his cloak to him against the night air. By the moonlight I could see that his skin was sallow, and his hair was long and thinning on top. I supposed him to be a gypsy, and I did not like the look of him.

The Giant stepped down into the path without a word or sound of warning. The little man gave a cry of astonishment and threw up his arm as if to ward off a blow. The Giant simply stood in the path with his arms folded over his broad chest, glowering down upon the intruder.

"Why have you come here?" the Giant demanded.

The man bowed, his hands tucked inside the front of his cloak. His face was a mask of terror. "Please," he said in a high-pitched, whining voice, "have mercy on me; have mercy, guardian of the woods…"

The Giant was unmoved. "State your business," he said.

The man began to babble, something about being lost and a merchant seeking fortune, but I did not hear his words. My eyes were fixed on his cloak. I did not like the way he kept his hands hidden. There was something wrong in his whole manner, something… feigned. My time in the woods with the Giant had taught me to trust a great deal to instinct, to pay attention to what my other senses knew that my eyes did not. What warned me first I do not know, but I became suddenly aware that the man had a knife in his cloak, and that he was carefully sizing up the Giant to determine how he would aim before throwing it, deceitfully and skillfully.

I shouted as loudly as I could and leaped from the ridge. I slammed into the man, knocking him to the ground, and punched him as hard as I could in the face. He shrieked with terror the whole while, and I grabbed him around the throat. I felt the Giant's hand on my shoulder, and turned to see him glaring at me.

"What are you thinking?" he asked.

In answer, I reached into the man's cloak. My fingers closed around the hilt of a knife. I pulled it out and held it up to the

Giant triumphantly. "He is a treacherous worm," I said. "He would have thrown it in a moment."

The Giant reached out slowly, and I handed the knife to him. My knees were still firmly planted in the dust on either side of the little man, and my hands were still around his throat, though loosely enough to let him breathe. The Giant examined the knife. He seemed shaken. I had never seen that look in his eyes. Itt frightened something deep inside of me, even as I felt wildly triumphant—I had saved the Angel of the Woods.

"Let him up," the Giant said. His voice was deeper than usual. Whether anger or some other emotion deepened it, I did not know. For a moment I considered disobeying him. But another look at the cowering weasel beneath me, his face smeared with his own blood, subdued the fire in my veins. He was not worth bothering over. I stood, wiping my hands together in a vain effort to clean them of dust and blood.

The Giant glared down at the intruder. "Get up," he said.

The little man scrambled to his feet, bowing and scraping and falling over himself as he backed away.

"Get out of my woods," the Giant said. "Never return. Do you understand me?"

"Oh yes, master," the man said, still bowing. "I understand."

We stood together and watched him hurry away into the gloom of the night. When at last the Giant turned to go, I thought his shoulders seemed stooped. For a moment he seemed to be a very old man.

"It is time to go home," he said. His voice was weary. I did not for a moment understand him. I thought he meant to return to whatever den he slept in—I never knew where it was—but as he continued down the road to the castle, understanding dawned.

"Do you mean that we're to go back to the Castle? I asked.

He looked back at me and nodded.

I felt a moment of elation. Back to the castle, place of beautiful mysteries. Back in the company of this man who had taught me so much, in whose defense I had proved myself—to myself— a hero. But elation was dulled by the sting of regret. I stood still in the path and closed my eyes, taking in the sound and feel of the night woods. They had become a part of me. Without realizing it, I had almost thought to stay within them forever. Yet another emotion overtook me at the thought: a pang of loneliness. Of fear. No, I could not stay here. It had been too long since I had spent much time in human company.

I opened my eyes. The Giant had also stopped, not much ahead of me. His eyes were lifted to the treetops and the moonlit sky above them. He turned back and looked at me from beneath his great black brows.

"Winter is coming," he said. "We will stay in the castle till spring."

Without another word he started down the path again. All in a confusion I followed, driven on by excitement and the fear of loneliness even as a part of me stayed behind to haunt the forest forever.

Chapter 9

———◆———

THE FIRST WINTER

SNOWFLAKES BEGAN TO FALL before we reached the castle, carried in on a deceptively light wind. They swirled around us in the darkness, catching the night lights like pieces of the moon. Heated by my victory, I now found myself fighting against the cold as the winter air blew against me and chilled the sweat on my body. I drew my fur cloak close as we stepped out from the trees. The grounds looked barren and desolate under the moonlight, and the castle sat white and ghostly amidst the falling snow.

It was late at night, and I wondered as we approached who would be awake to welcome us. I needn't have wondered. Only minutes after the Angel's knock the great wooden door swung open, and Nora stood in the torchlight. She wore a long white robe over her nightclothes, and her hair was down, falling to her waist. The torchlight made its golden waves deepen in colour. Perhaps it was the cold that heightened my senses, but I felt that I had never seen Nora before. The blue of her eyes, usually so sharp, was softened by a mix of concern and welcome—the welcome, I knew, was all for the Angel. Standing in the doorway Nora looked to me wondrous and magical, an ancient fairy queen still garbed in the beauty of youth, ushering us into her otherworldly castle. What happened to my heart in that moment is beyond my power to explain, even now.

She bid us enter in low tones, her torch casting strange shadows on the flagstones as she closed the door behind us. Her eyes swept over both of us, and she addressed herself to me while looking at the Angel.

"Your hands are bloody," she said. "What happened?"

The Angel grunted as he removed his cloak and laid it on the bench. "An intruder," he said. "Nothing out of the ordinary."

Nora cast another glance at me, but apparently she was satisfied with the Angel's answer. I was not. I waited for him to give some nod to what I had done for him, but he said nothing. He merely finished removing his outdoor clothing and looked at me with his dark eyes.

"Go off to bed, boy," he said. "There is work to be done on the morrow."

I had many things I wanted to say, but I bit the words back and turned to go. I had not ascended three steps when I was seized with a sudden desire to see Nora again, to talk to her, to make something of myself in her eyes. I turned back and peered through the crack of the door to the hall. The Giant was still there. Nora was with him. His great arms were folded gently around her shoulders, and her head rested on his chest—like a child in her father's embrace. He was speaking to her, but his words were no more to me than a low rumble. Once again I turned and began the slow trudge up to my room.

I awoke late in the morning to the sound of running feet and chattering voices. Some of the gaggle had chosen the landing and stairs outside my door to set up a cascading doll village. The small window in my room revealed a dismal landscape, only half-visible through the slanting snow. The sky was slate grey and seemingly untinged by sunlight. Winter had come with missional passion and was saying its morning prayers upon us all, devoting itself to the task of burying the whole world under snow and wind and cloud.

I paced beneath my window for a little while, sitting down at last in a high-backed wooden chair facing into the room. I felt strangely disquieted. I had grown accustomed to my forest den, but I knew that even that had been swallowed and transformed by the storm. I was not eager to face the house or anyone in it.

I had not been sitting long before my stomach began to complain aloud of ill-treatment. I welcomed its discomfort at first as a general reflection of my mood, but hunger eventually got the better of me. I dressed and left the room, wading precariously through the gaggle and their dolls on my way to the kitchen. An iron pot sat simmering on the stove with the dregs of porridge left in it, growing stiff and yellow. The household, I gathered, had eaten. I helped myself to the porridge, bathing it in milk and brown sugar in an attempt to make the best of it, and ate by myself at the long wooden table with my feet propped impolitely up on the chair beside me.

Nora whisked into the kitchen when I was nearly finished my breakfast, arms full of firewood, her hair tied up in a bun. She dropped the firewood into the bin beside the stove, cranked open the iron door, and tossed in a couple of logs, jabbing the whole mess with an iron poker that made sparks fly. Finished, she straightened up, wiped her hands on her apron, and looked at me with something akin to amusement in her eyes.

"Spirit's gone with the sun?" she asked. "The storm will end soon enough, believe me. And then there'll be work for you, so be glad of your ease now."

The fairy queen was gone, replaced by the brusque house mother I had never warmed to. I was in no mood for condescension, and I am ashamed to say that I nearly answered her back. But just then two very little girls burst through the kitchen door, bounding and bubbling with noise. The smallest one catapulted herself straight at Nora. Nora caught the little thing up in her strong arms and held her close. She smiled as the child shyly hid her face in her neck. The other child was tugging at her apron, so Nora lowered herself down and listened, her face patient and open, a smile still playing on her lips. She balanced on her heels while the little one snuggled closer.

For all that the wind howled outside, I thought that the heart of sunlight and fire-warmth had come into the kitchen and settled over Nora. No, she wasn't a fairy queen… but for the first time in my life, I became aware that there was something deep inside woman that was more beautiful than magic could ever be. And, also for the first time in my life, I wondered how any young man could ever be hero enough to deserve to plumb the depths.

Nora was right. There was work to be done. When after three days the storm ceased and the sun came out, I found myself neverendingly patching this bit of roof against the melting snow, and plugging that hole or crack against the cold wind, or clearing this or that path of snow—four back-breaking feet of it in the drifts—so that the girls could get where they needed to go.

The sun had not been up one hour on that first day before Nora announced that my help was needed at the river. She dragged me out into the stinging cold of the morning, along with the Pixie and two of the older children, that I might shovel clear a large patch of ice. I then used the shovel to put a hole in the surface so the girls could gather water for the day in their metal buckets. And so little could I bear to be useless while they lugged pails of icy water back to the house, that I put down my shovel and used my back and arms to relieve the two older children of their burdens. The Pixie praised me for this in her laughing way, while Nora commented that once I had done this twice every day, I shouldn't slop so much of the water on my legs—which would be better, both for the water and for my legs. It would be better also for the kitchen, which would soon begin to smell if my trousers needed to be hung over the stove to dry every morning. But I thought that her eyes were friendlier when she looked at me. The general unflappable calm about her was happy and not sullied by my presence.

When the storm had been relegated to the memory of a week or two, the winter quieted down for a time. Much of the snow melted off. I had no time to be glad of the respite, for as soon as the landscape was navigable, the Angel led an expedition to the western edge of the woods. Twelve of us went to work with a vengeance, chopping and hacking at the trees until we had enough firewood, I thought, to melt the mountaintops. That is, the Angel and I chopped and hacked. The rest of the delegation, led by a splendidly pink-cheeked Pixie in her fur-trimmed coat of royal blue, stripped the trees of their branches and twigs and carted the wood back to the castle. They sang while they worked, and threw an inordinate number of snowballs, until enough snow had trickled down the back of my coat to make me think that article of apparel practically worthless.

I inquired of the Pixie, on that first fine winter's day, with the sun sparkling blindingly on the white lawns, whether the Poet's genius also disqualified him from chopping wood. She seemed surprised at my question.

"The Poet is a creature of the summer," she told me. "He is not here now."

And indeed, I did not see him, not through all the long months of winter. His presence was now and then missed, especially as I sometimes wished for another of my sex to engage when Nora chased me out of the kitchen or the Pixie was particularly inexplicable, or when the giggling outside my door grew too much to bear and I stepped one too many times on the doll furniture strewn about the stairs and nearly broke my neck trying to get my balance again.

The Angel was there every day, a great dark presence in the house, magnificent in his usual silence. The children loved him and would climb all over him whenever he sat down, but though he listened to them prattle away at him for hours, he rarely had anything to say in return. They did not seem to mind. The love in his eyes, surrounded by deep creases of laughter and care, was enough of an answer for them.

Chapter 10

FURS

UPON A MIDWINTER'S DESCENT to the cellar, in search of a middling sack of cocoa, it occured to me that the castle's stores were running low. The dried things hanging from the low ceiling were nearly depleted; the vegetables buried in underground nooks just as sparse; flour, sugar, and molasses all dwindling. Porridge there was in abundance, but even the children had begun to revolt against its frequent appearances.

I climbed the cramped stairway back up to the kitchen, intending to inform Nora of this alarming development, but I found that her omniscience had not failed her. Her head was bent over a list on the kitchen table, which she rapidly scratched at with a quill and ink, making calculations. The Angel and the Pixie stood on either side of her, now and again making some suggestion, all three frowning as only those who are trying to manipulate numbers do frown. Half a dozen pots simmered on the iron stove behind them, making the room uncomfortably warm.

"It will do," Nora said at last, pushing herself back from the table. "If we sell them all, there is enough to tide us through the winter."

The Pixie laughed. "Well, don't be too optimistic about it," she said. "It's a splendid haul, Nora, and you know it."

Nora looked at her friend placidly, wiping her forehead with the back of her hand and leaving a slight streak of ink across it. "It will do, as I said."

"It will more than do," the Pixie declared, looking down at the paper again. "Let *me* do the haggling, and we'll make a Christmas of it. See if we don't."

I strode forward and laid the cocoa on the table, drawing attention from the three at last. "If there is haggling to be done," I said, "leave it to me. I could haggle a man out of his only winter coat for less than he paid for it."

The Pixie laughed. "But can you haggle him into one, and out of his money?" she asked.

"What are we selling?" I asked, straining for a look at the paper. It was smudged and dirty, written upon in a broad hand that was difficult to make out, with Nora's long narrow figures at the bottom.

The Angel answered me. "Furs," he said.

Nora looked up at me. "Have you ever tried to sell anything?"

"I told you," I said. "I'm an expert."

"He'll go with you," the Angel decided. "He can be your protector."

"And I'll do all the real work," the Pixie said. "You know I sell more than anyone else. And buy more, too."

Nora's face seemed to cloud a little. "I think you should stay home this year," she said. "They're getting to know you too well."

"What if they do?" the Pixie asked. "I have been cooped up here all winter."

"We all have," Nora said. Her eyes flashed. Their obvious disagreement made me uncomfortable, especially as this hardly seemed like an isolated conversation.

The Pixie flushed and looked away. "I know you think I attract too much attention," she said. "But I can't help that. And I *can't* stay here all winter, Nora; you know I can't."

In reply Nora simply looked at the Angel. His eyes were troubled as he regarded both of them. His answer was a long time in coming. He stood as he answered. "You will both go," he said. He nodded in my direction. "And Hawk."

Nora opened her mouth again. "I would rather not—" she began.

The Angel cut her off. "Go," he said. "You'll be needed."

Nora did not look up. "Yes, sir," she said.

The Angel left the kitchen. The Pixie followed, after a concerned glance at Nora.

I cleared my throat. "Surely it isn't that—"

Nora stood abruptly. "Excuse me," she said. She left me standing alone in the kitchen, sweating slightly in the heat of the overworked iron stove, and entirely at a loss for what to do with the cocoa.

———❖———

I trekked out into the woods two days later, following the Angel's footsteps through the snow. Together we journeyed deep into the forest's embrace, down paths that had once been familiar but now were changed. Winter had entered the woods and made me once again a stranger in them. Beneath the cold and snow and deathly stillness, I knew that my woods still existed. My den was still under the roots of an old tree in another part of the forest. The birds and animals would return before long, or else they were still here—sleeping, waiting for spring to call them out again.

I did not like the change, and I said nothing as we walked.

Snowflakes drifted lightly down around us. The Angel looked over his shoulder at me. He smiled slightly through his great dark beard.

"It has not changed," he said. "The heart of the woods is the same in every season."

"I am inclined to dislike the seasons," I said. "They make a foreigner of me, and I was at home here."

"Do you begrudge the woods their depth?" the Angel asked, looking ahead once again. His voice was clear in the still air. "Are you unhappy because there is more to them than you saw at first?"

I looked up toward the treetops. "I thought I knew them," I said. "It only took months."

"Here," the Angel said, stopping abruptly before a tangle of small trees. Even without leaves, their small branches were laced so closely together as to make a nearly impenetrable screen. I stopped in confusion. We were in search of the Angel's furhouse, and so I had expected to go to a part of the woods I had never visited before—after all, in my months in the woods I had never suspected the existence of such a place. But I had been here many times, or thought I had.

The Angel paid no mind to my confusion. He reached into the thicket and pulled a heavy door open. I could see it now: grey and low to the ground was a rough-hewn hut. It was dark within, and I followed the Angel down a set of steps to the sunken floor. The walls stretched up nine feet on either side; high enough for the Angel to stand at his full height and look comfortable. He lit a candle, and the flames flickered and danced on the colours and textures of the furs that hung on the walls: fox red and badger black, beaver brown and rabbit grey.

He looked at me with his eyes smiling. "When a thing is truly worth knowing," he said, "you will find it takes a lifetime to know it."

Chapter 11

———◆◆———

IN THE TOWN

THE PIXIE, NORA, AND I LEFT the castle on a cold November morning, on a small horsecart heaped with furs. Nora relinquished the reins to me without too much trouble before we left. She nestled among the furs with the Pixie while I drove the cart over the frozen road through the woods. A thin layer of snow lay on the ground all around us, and the sun shone freely through the bare tree branches. I could see my breath in the air. With the leather reins in my hand and the rumble of the wheels on the earth, the clop of the shaggy pony's hooves before me and the voices of Nora and the Pixie behind me, I thought it was a good morning to be alive.

The woods were still and barren, but somewhere in their midst the Giant walked again, haunting the landscape. He had taken to patrolling the woods as soon as the snow had melted enough to encourage travelers. He returned to the castle when the weather grew fiercest, and wandered the forest when it gentled, but he did not ask me to accompany him. I wondered why, but I did not ask.

We rode all morning, out from the woods and over the hills toward a town I had never seen. Nora directed me now and again, but she needn't have. The pony knew where it wanted to go. We came at last over the crest of a high hill to see the town laid out before us, and both Nora and the Pixie climbed up from their places to lean over my shoulders and see the settlement that was at once familiar and foreign to them. I knew that they had been here before—Nora to trade and the Pixie to be curious and arouse curiosity—but their castle world was far removed from any such place. It was a large town, big enough to house both goodman and reprobate. The nobility of the province lived some way off, in a great house on lands far larger, if less wild and beautiful, than the lawns of the castle. The Pixie had learned as much by asking questions and by reading books in the library that gave some of the area's history, and she was glad to share her knowledge with me.

The town, it seemed, was located at a crossroads between various larger settlements, and so it made a fair resting place for tinkers, vagabonds, circuses, and all manner of passers-through. Its central location ensured it was not cut off from the rest of the world when the cold weather came, and so the town had made a habit, owing both to its number of visitors and to its number of wintering merchants, of holding a market several times every month. It was a perfect place for the inhabitants of the castle to sell their wares. And so they had been doing, I gathered, for some years.

The wide main street of the town was already buzzing with activity as we made our furred way into the midst of the market. Nora soon spotted an open place, and we pulled into it. The girls jumped off the cart and pulled handmade wooden stands out from beneath it, which they had collapsed and tied onto the wagon with stout twine.

All around us the heady atmosphere of the town filled my senses. Coins and horse tack jangled, hooves and wheels stamped and creaked through the streets. Voices called from a thousand wooden cloaks and shawls and hoods and leather coats. I was overwhelmed by the sense of being *out*, of being among mankind again. Everything here seemed earthier, more real than anything at the castle. Here were men wearing muddy leather boots, with swords and tools strapped to their belts and worn gloves covering their hands. Here were voices of every pitch and tone, gruff and smooth, haughty and loud, shy and retiring, young and old. Here were hags and hagglers; wealthy men and beggars; voices raised in praise and in argument. I could smell beer and hot sausage, horse dung and rawhide. The air was vaporous with the breath of men and horses, and with smoke and steam from off the cooking fires where sausages, breads, and deep fried rolls of raisin dough filled the air with their scents.

I was intoxicated by it all. I heard voices raised in anger and suddenly my heart was pounding. All my old instincts were awake, and I longed to join the fight and exchange a few good-natured blows. The Pixie, too, watched the passing crowds with a kind of hunger in her eyes. Only Nora seemed unaffected. She worked to get the furs in good display, and then almost immediately she was taking and counting money for them, arguing price in low, gentle tones with an old woman who did not look as though she could have afforded a bundle of rags. The old woman left with a grey fox fur, and I wondered what Nora had accepted for it.

It was the shopowners' attention Nora really wanted, and it wasn't long before she had it. For all the dizzying humanity in the streets, not many paid us a second glance, and I soon felt useless. Our little corner was in capable hands. I wandered away into the crowd. Dimly I remembered the Giant's intent that I play protector to my companions, and so I made a point of staying near enough to the cart that I would hear them if they called.

Among the tents and stands and pony carts that made up

the market a few more permanent buildings stood. The busiest of these was a tavern. It had been months since I had last had a drop of beer to warm myself, and I wanted it now. I walked into a haze of pipe smoke and tobacco, through which men shouted and laughed, and someone in a back corner was singing, off-key and a little off-colour.

I knew very well how threadbare my pockets were and that a drink was never to be had for nothing. Still, I hoped to convince the tavern-keeper that I would pay for it, one way or another, on a better day.

A big burly man with a red beard squinted at me through the darkness and waved his hand. "Away with ye," he said. "I've no time to trouble with penniless beggars."

I drew myself up. "I am no beggar, sir," I said. "I am the son of a nobleman."

He looked at me out of a half-cocked eye, his lip partly pulled up from his teeth. "And I'm the son of the almighty khan," he said. "Get off!"

There were men in the tavern attuned to his words. In minutes I was unceremoniously thrown back into the cold air. I half-landed, half-rolled in the street, near a narrow ditch where refuse and dirty, melted snow flowed together. A pair of rats skittered and fought over something old and once-edible near my head, uncaring that the boots of a hundred men trod all around them. As I raised myself to my knee, my eyes scanned the crowd—and zeroed in on a face I knew. A rat's face.

The gypsy from the woods.

I had unfinished business with the rogue. I scrambled to my feet and shouted. "You there!"

He turned and saw me. His expression changed from its usual sly and cunning look to one so vile and condescending that I could not bear it. I threw myself at him and bowled him to the ground.

The Gypsy curled up and covered his head with his arms as I rained blows upon him, demanding apologies, explanations, some balm to my much wounded pride and pent up anger. He shrieked like the coward he was, and suddenly I felt hands on my arms and shoulders and waist, and I was being dragged away.

"Let me go!" I shouted, struggling against the hold of the townsmen. "The wretch! He is up to no good, I tell you! A murderer!"

I whirled around. A large black carriage blocked out the sky just behind me. Guards in purple livery stood sternly around it, and I saw that the men who now held me wore the same uniform. An imposing grey head, belonging to a woman of impossible age with a dragon's mien and a sharp eye with which she now regarded me, leaned out of the window.

"On what grounds do you accuse him, young man?" the woman asked.

Her voice, her entire bearing, demanded that I answer. I wrenched my arms free of the guards and crossed them, meeting the woman's glare with one of my one. "He tried to kill the Giant of the Woods," I said.

Chapter 12

———◆◆———

LADY BRAWNLYN

THE WOMAN STEPPED DOWN from the carriage, imposing in her regality. Despite her evident age she stood straight and strong. She was taller than I, and I felt dirty and exposed before her eyes. She wore all black, from the covering of black lace on her head to the shoes on her feet. It was the traditional garb of a widow, but richly made and proudly worn. The guards stepped back and inclined their heads as her feet touched the ground, and she strode forward with her cane in her hand until she was close enough to tower over me.

"A great mystery," she said. "You accuse this man—" she pointed to the gypsy, still lying on the ground, with the end of her silver-tipped cane—"of attempting to murder a man who is not here present. A man whose existence I have long been given to doubt. And who are *you* to make such wild claims? Defend yourself well, for all I can see is a troublemaking scrap of a boy."

During this speech the gypsy raised himself from the ground, casting furtive, hopeful glances from the widow to myself and nervously wringing his hands. I could hardly bear it.

"I am the son of a nobleman," I answered, and I gave the name of the province wherein my father's estate lay. The guards looked at each other with a new air of respect for me, which I was gratified to notice. "I claim what I know to be true, for I was with the Giant when this creature attacked him, by stealth and artifice and without provocation."

"Do you then *know* this man?" the widow asked. "This Giant of the Woods who gives so many cause to fear?"

"I do," I answered. "He is a good man. I have trained with him, all this fall and winter."

The widow nodded, the signs of thought playing across her face. Then she looked down at the gypsy, who cringed away from her. "You," she barked. "Does this young man speak truth?"

"Please, your ladyship," the gypsy answered. "I am a man who will defend myself when I am attacked, and the Giant did attack me without cause."

The widow raised her eyebrow with disdain. "A man who will defend himself, indeed," she said. "You are a coward. Only a moment ago you lay shrieking on the ground while this boy pummeled you. Every eye here saw it."

The gypsy ducked his head as the guards and the gathering crowd tittered with laughter. His loathsome head turned crimson beneath his thinning hair.

"Your humiliation is punishment enough for cowardice," the widow continued, "but you are here on charges far more serious. Guards!" She turned, calling several of her men to attention. "The law must inquire further into this matter," she said. "Escort our friend to the gaol and tell the sheriff what has here transpired."

"Yes, my lady," the chief of the guards answered. Unceremoniously they hauled my opponent away. I watched him with go with mingled pleasure and disappointment, for now he was quite out of my hands.

"Now, young man," the widow said, her attention fully back to me. "If you will be so kind as to help me back into my carriage, I would like a word with you."

I stepped forward and offered her my hand, aware that I was being honoured. When she was seated comfortably again in her coach, she called me up after her.

I settled into the padded black seat opposite the widow, letting the opulence of the coach sink in and bring back memories of my old life. It seemed a lifetime ago that I had belonged to the world of nobility. I had never intended to leave it entirely—only to seek my own fortune, to make a name for myself, and to return home a great man. My adventures had thus far been very different than I had anticipated. Seated in the widow's coach, surrounded by the scent and feel of riches, I suddenly felt closer to my goal than ever I had since I had first entered the woods.

"Do you know who I am?" the widow asked me.

I nodded, drawing on the history lesson the Pixie had given me. "I suppose you to be the Lady Brawnlyn," I said, "mistress of a very great estate in these parts."

She nodded. "You are correct in your suppositions. I am mistress of a very great estate indeed—this town and the towns outlying all belong to me. My late husband acquired great wealth and lands before he died. He ruled them well." A shadow passed over her face. "Though there has been… some trouble in our borders."

"I am sorry to hear it," I said.

She smiled a thin-lipped smile. "You may perhaps be of help," she said. "I have been in need of someone like you."

I was surprised, and did not attempt to hide it. "If I can be of assistance to you, madam, by all means call upon me. I am surprised to hear that you have no one."

"I am a wealthy woman," she answered me, "but not in descendants, nor in trust. I have one daughter, no sons. I do not trust my guards. They are what they are… but I need something of better stock."

"As I said," I answered, "I will be of help in any way that I can."

She smiled, the same joyless, no-nonsense smile. "I am glad to hear it," she said. "I will see you in my house this day next week. I shall send a coach and four for you. Where do you live?"

I shifted my feet uncomfortably. "If you please, ma'am," I said, "I would rather come on my own."

She raised her eyebrows and nodded. "Very well. I will see you after the noon meal."

With little more in the way of ceremony I was dismissed, and the Widow Brawnlyn rode away in a great clatter of dust and wheels. The townspeople parted before her. They paid her homage by doffing their caps and muttering to themselves.

I had by now been gone some time, and when I made my way back to the fur stand Nora greeted me with stormy eyes. "Where have you been?" she asked.

I bristled. "Things have happened," I answered, intending to go into detail.

"Yes, they have," Nora said. "For example? I have sold all my furs, without help. And the Pixie has disappeared. In all of your wanderings, you wouldn't happen to have seen her?"

Chapter 13

———

THE WIDOW'S COMMISSION

THE PIXIE SAVED ME THE NEED to answer by appearing at that very moment, wrapped in her dark winter cloak. With a nod to the two of us she began to take down the wooden stands Nora had used to display the furs.

Nora voice held a warning note. "Pixie..."

The Pixie looked up from her work. Her eyes were pleading. "I went to see a friend, Nora, that is all," she said.

Nora sighed. Her face, like the Pixie's, was full of emotion, but I could not read it. "Why should you defend yourself?" she asked at last.

Without another word she bent down beside the Pixie and got to work. Neither one of them was happy. The Pixie's face was flushed, perhaps with shame, perhaps with the stubborn elation of having been out and free against everyone's wishes to the contrary. I did not flatter myself that I knew her so well I could tell the difference.

The wooden stands were heavy, so I volunteered to tie them back on to the bottom of the wagon. Nora went to tend to the horse while I did so, and the Pixie bent down beside me.

"I saw it all," she whispered. "What trouble are you in?"

I nearly hit my head on the bottom of the wagon, so surprised was I. The Pixie's tone was stern and not a little threatening. I had never pegged her for a blackmailer, but I knew now that my secret might very well cost me. And secret it was. Until that moment I did not know it, but I did not want anyone from the castle—Nora, or the Giant especially—to know what had happened, or what had come of it.

I peered out from under the wagon at the Pixie's exquisite face, shadowed by her cloak and the mischief that hung axe-like over my head. "No trouble at all," I rasped, trying to whisper and not doing terribly well at it. "Everything has been nicely settled."

The Pixie raised an eyebrow and whispered back, "That woman was the Widow Brawnlyn. A noblewoman!"

I grew annoyed. "And I am a nobleman's son."

The Pixie leaned a little closer and lowered her voice even more. "The Angel won't care much about that."

Nora rounded the wagon at that moment and I banged my head on the side of wagon as I clambered to my feet. I shot the Pixie a warning look. She replied by folding her arms and smiling smugly. I thanked my lucky stars that she was standing behind Nora, where the expression on her face couldn't be seen by anyone but me.

As we were ready to go, I headed back to the front of the wagon. Somehow Nora made it there before me and snatched up the reins. "I'll drive," she said. There was enough question in her voice to flatter me a little… she *was* asking. I nodded and climbed into the back, made far more unwelcoming by the absence of furs to cushion its wooden sides. The Pixie climbed in after me and leaned against the opposite side of the cart as Nora clucked to the pony with a snap of the reins. We started down the road, through the town and back toward the castle.

"Not a word," I hissed.

"No," the Pixie said back. "Not a word."

I was content. I would go to the Widow Brawnlyn in seven days, as I had promised. The Pixie would not give me away… but I knew that I would eventually pay for her silence.

<hr />

I left the castle while the Giant was out. The sun was climbing in the sky. The woods were cold but bright in the late morning light. I had some understanding of the Giant's habits from the time I had spent with him in the woods and was thus fairly certain I knew how to miss him, both as I went out and as I returned. Nora was busy with the children as I left. Three had engaged her in an argument of sorts while a smaller one pulled on her skirt and begged for a drink. She barely had a harried nod to spare me when I announced that I was going hunting.

The crisp air greeted me, rife with adventure. I drank it in with every step I took, my old cudgel resting on my shoulder. I felt tremendously alive. Every sense was standing at readiness. The danger of meeting the Giant in the woods, and thus being forced to an explanation I did not want to give, only heightened my enjoyment of the day. The widow had recognized my worth. Her summons had told me that I was to be a hero at last, and I felt myself to be one—every inch of me.

I was out of the woods ere long. In the town where I had first met the Pixie, I found the blacksmith on his way to the great house of the Family Brawnlyn. I convinced him to take me along, and as we journeyed I sat beside him and drank in the countryside. It grew tamer as we neared the mansion. The woods were fewer; the fields broad and pastoral. The flat landscape made me think of the moors around my own home and reminded me once again that I was at last taking steps to fulfill my destiny. Why I put so much stock in the Widow's summons I cannot now say; but then it seemed to me that she opened the door to the world.

The mansion itself was a dark grey edifice, veined with climbing vines that in the summer would burst into the green of ivy leaves, but which were now a dead brown. There were gardens all around the house, well-kept but full of strange, wild things, frozen in the twisted mien of winter. I learned later that it was the Widow's taste to surround herself with that which was wild and dark; with that which suggested danger. A wide stone drive led through the weird gardens to a pair of high oak doors, above which the heads of gargoyles leered down. It was an old house and the stonework was grim and imposing.

There was activity about the place, but it was subdued. A flock of crows on a low stone wall flapped as someone disturbed them beyond the left side of the house. The blacksmith took himself away to the stables on the right. I walked alone, like a vagabond with my stick over my shoulder, up the drive to the oak doors.

Hardly had I knocked when the doors swung inward and a servant bid me enter. He led me across a polished floor of grey marble toward another set of doors. We had not yet reached them when I felt eyes on me. I turned to look around the sweeping greatness of the room. A magnificent staircase curved up toward the gloom of the upper stories like a road leading into the clouds, and on it stood a young woman: dark, stormy, and strikingly beautiful. My heart moved at the sight of her, and for a moment I couldn't breathe. Her presence was commanding, yet there was something cold in the eyes as she descended the staircase, holding her hand out to me. I took the slender fingers and bent to kiss her hand. Even as I did, the Widow Brawnlyn stepped out of the shadows.

"My daughter, Lady Genevieve Brawnlyn," she said.

I looked up at the beautiful face and said, "My lady." Genevieve nodded in reply, and turned her eyes to her mother. I followed suit.

"I am glad to see you here," the Widow said.

"I told you I would come," I said.

"Yes," she answered, holding out her hand that I might pay homage to her as I had to her daughter. "But not every young man is as good as his word. I thought you were. I am glad to see that I was correct."

"Your judgement is fine," I answered. The Widow seemed pleased. She gestured toward the sitting room from whence she had come, just off the grand hall. "Let us sit," she said.

We entered the room together, the butler a shadow at our heels. He bore a silver tray with various delicacies. The Widow settled into a cushioned chair, its ornately carved arms glowing red and gold in the light of the oil lamps. The drapes were drawn; there was no natural light in the room. Genevieve sat beside her mother and did not say a word. There was another chair on the other side of the Widow, and here that grand lady indicated that I should sit. I did, and leaned forward, caught up in the mysterious aspect of the room and its inhabitants.

"Please, my lady," I said. "Tell me why you have called me here. Your hospitality is gracious, but you said I could be of assistance to you."

The Widow smiled, barely. She unfurled a fan of darkest red and fanned herself with it. "Yes," she said. "Tell me, young man. Have you any experience at arms?"

I nodded. "As every young nobleman does. I can quit myself well in any contest."

"And in leading men?" she asked. "You seem like a leader."

I did not tell her that for nearly two seasons now I had been first a loner in the forest and then a water-carrier for a houseful of girls. I had, once or twice before I left home, been respected by other young men like myself who trained together in the ways of the higher classes. I affirmed her suspicion that I could indeed lead others.

"Tell me," she said. "What do you know about this province of mine?"

I looked down at the rich carpet. "Very little, I'm afraid," I said. "I have been confined to one small piece of it nearly since my arrival. It seems to me a very rich land. Very beautiful."

Something flickered in the Widow's eye. "Yes," she said. "It is very beautiful. A magnificent inheritance. But it is also a wild place. We are not far from the outer reaches of our country, and across those borders people are uncivilized, treacherous. Much of their character has come across the border and infected my lands. We have always been known for the wealth of the land, but equally we are known for the vile things that transpire here. Other provinces have legendary heroes. Here, despite the work my husband and his fathers did to keep the land settled, we are plagued by legendary villains. Thieves. They haunt the forests and roam at night."

She was not finished. I had grown uncomfortable; my hands clammy. I was not sure why.

"Since my husband died things have grown steadily worse," the Widow said. "My daughter and I are in need of a man to help us tame the province again."

"Have—have you had no one in all these years?" I stammered.

She looked at me shrewdly. "Oh, there are men," she said. "But no one of noble birth. No one with the strength and resolve to make his mark here. No one we could welcome as… one of us." Her eyes went to Genevieve, whose beauty was as distracting as it was cold.

I understood at once what she was getting at. Genevieve Brawnlyn was a beautiful young woman, but there were few prospects in this part of the world—few men who could be trusted to take lordship over the province. The Widow's words swirled in my head. This was a place without heroes. And the Widow and her daughter, rulers over the land, were looking to me.

I swallowed, regaining my composure. "I will be of service to you," I said, "in any way I can." I looked up inadvertently, and my eyes locked with the stormy grey of Genevieve's. Deliberately I turned back to the Widow, who was ready with a commission.

"There is, in the woods north of here, a band of robbers who have made the road notoriously dangerous for all travellers. I want you to take a band of my guards and rout them from the forest. Bring them back to my prisons or have done with them in some other way, but I want them driven from my land. They are bloodthirsty men; you need have no qualms about dealing with them. My spies can tell you precisely where to find them. Will you do this?"

I stood. "I will," I said.

Chapter 14

———◆———

THE WIDOW'S DAUGHTER

I RODE OUT AT THE HEAD of the Widow's men not two hours later. They were uniformed in grey: sharp, imposing figures. Before them I rode like a rogue warrior, without uniform to identify me with any cause but my own, flushed with all that the ride could mean to me. I bade the Widow—and her daughter—goodbye as the tall black horse they had lent me pranced impatiently beneath me. With a shout and a slap of the reins, I gave the horse its freedom. We were off. We vanquished the stone drive in mere minutes, and with the men whooping behind me and the hooves of their horses tearing up the road, we charged on the north woods.

I signalled for the men to quiet themselves as we approached the woodland border. When we plunged into the forest world we were as silent as a band of men on horseback can be. I knew where to go. Lady Brawnlyn's spy had given me detailed directions, but even if he had not, I would have had no trouble finding the bandits. I could read the forest. I knew what tracks were man-made and which were the marks of beasts or the tricks of nature. I could see signs of the men's presence everywhere.

The robbers had made their headquarters inside a cave, hewn out of a rock that rose from the ground like the head of a great serpent. My eyes caught sight of its dark opening. I signalled to the men to fan out behind me, that we might approach the cave mouth from every angle. I rode ahead, into the clearing alone. The strong odour of revelry washed out from the cave's dark maw: wine, meat, and the stink of drunkenness. I reigned in my horse and called out in a loud voice, "Ho, there! Come out and face justice!"

I heard a shuffling and low muttering in the cave, and then a filthy man appeared in the opening. The hair he had hung long and scraggly down the back of his neck. He leaned on the side of the cave and eyed me with one yellow eye.

"And who might you be?" he asked.

"I am called Hawk," I told him. "I am come in the name of the Lady Brawnlyn to see that your thievery is stopped."

The man looked up at me with an indescribable sneer. "Is that so?" he asked. He half turned and called into the cave. "Come out, boys, and see the whelp the Widow has sent us!"

Even as he spoke, he drew a broadsword out from the darkness of the cave and lunged at me. He had given me little warning, yet it was as though I had already studied his every move. It was nothing to me to meet the sword, to disarm him, to ride on the others who came forth from the cave. I gave a battle cry as my men poured out of the forest. The fight was over almost before it had begun. I knew that I had acted swiftly; strongly. I knew that I looked in the eyes of every man there like a hero. When I look back now, I know that it was the Giant's training that enabled me to fight as I did, but I spared no thought for him then.

We tied the robbers and threw them over the backs of our horses like so many sacks of grain. The filthy man who had come out to meet me at the mouth of the cave rode behind me with his arms tied behind his back, and all the way he spewed curses and accusations from his mouth. I sat straighter, prouder, as I thought of the life this man had led and the way I had ended it.

We entered the town. All the people gathered to gawk at us from the sides of the road. Someone recognized the bandits and shouted out news of what we had done. The townspeople cheered, and I thought that my heart could not beat more proudly. A small part of me whispered that the Giant and all his fair host should be here to see me, but at the same time I did not think they would be pleased. The Giant, I thought, cared only for his small world. Ah, but had I not protected that world also by doing away with the bandits? And might I not someday reign over that world, if in the years to come the Widow should look favourably on me?

The low voice of the filthy bandit intruded on my thoughts, audible under the cheers of the gathering crowd. "What did she promise you, eh?" he asked. "What? Money? Or that daughter of hers?" The man laughed, his laugh like gravel in my ears. "She did, didn't she? Offered you the whole world, young fool. All for the cause of ridding the forest of me."

We had reached the gaol. I had no more patience for the man. I dismounted and hauled him down roughly. Within the hour the bandits were locked safely away, and I was once more on horseback, headed again for the house of Widow Brawnlyn.

———⟫◆⟪———

It was evening when I rode up the drive at the head of my small band of men. They dispersed behind me as I dismounted, and a boy came to lead my horse away. I patted its sleek black neck, my eyes all the time on the doors of the house. I was eager to give account for my actions.

The butler led me again to a well-furnished sitting room, where I was surprised to find, not two ladies waiting for me, but three. My surprise was doubled when I recognized in the third the face of the Pixie. She looked up at me, tea cup in her hand, without a trace of guilt on her smooth brow. She was seated next to Genevieve. They contrasted like fire and storm. I was not sure I had ever seen so much loveliness in one place.

The Widow greeted me with a nod of her aged head. "Reports have already reached me," she said. "A rider came in from the town. I could not be more pleased."

I nodded. A flush of colour stole into my cheeks. Genevieve had her strange grey eyes fixed on me, and I could not help but remember at what future her mother had hinted.

"I shall call for you again," the Widow said. "Is this agreeable to you?"

I answered yes. I was flattered. Flattered that she treated me with deference; flattered that she considered me a help; flattered by the way her daughter looked at me. And I was inordinately pleased that it was all done in front of the Pixie, who had only seen me as laundry-toter and water boy before this—the Pixie! I glared at her. Flattered I was, but I would have liked to wring her neck. How on earth had she come to be there?

Lady Brawnlyn gestured the Pixie's way. She had not asked me to sit, so I stood, hot and without any idea of what I would say if the Widow inquired after my friend's audacity.

"You did not tell us that you had brought a young lady with you," Lady Brawnlyn said. "A charming creature—utterly delightful. Next time you must not be so remiss in introducing your friends."

What could I say? I stammered an apology and dutifully promised to bring her with me when next I came. We left together, the Pixie's arm in mine as I escorted her over the drive. "How did you come here?" I hissed once we were out of earshot.

The Pixie smiled sweetly at me—well aware that we were not yet out of eyeshot. "I followed you," she said. "Not a word to Nora or the Angel."

"I'm not a fool," I answered.

I looked back at the house then. Genevieve Brawnlyn was standing in the open doors, her dark hair stirred by the wind.

Her eyes haunted me all the way back to the Castle.

Chapter 15

INDEPENDENCE

I SPOKE WITH THE PIXIE as we walked the roads through the town together. It seemed she had not intended to present herself at the house: only to wander the grounds, and, if questioned, to explain that she had come with me. She was caught in short order, as only someone as vividly conspicuous as the Pixie could be, and stood almost immediately in the good graces of Widow Brawnlyn and her daughter. They had insisted that she come back to see them.

I allowed this information to flatter me. The Pixie had come in my name and been welcomed with open arms. I wondered how they would have welcomed her had she gone to them in the Giant's name alone. I knew well enough that if the Pixie found herself a favourite of the noble family she had only her own charms to thank for it—but at least I had opened the door. We crept through the darkwood together, under the evening sky, lost in our own thoughts. The Pixie seemed apprehensive as we neared the Castle. As before, we had neatly avoided the Giant's detection. I felt sorry for her. She was all but locked up in that castle, I thought—a flower trying to grow in a world without enough sun. We parted ways in the woods. She returned home in the fading light while I spent a few hours in the woods—hunting, as I had told Nora I would do. What the Pixie told Nora I never knew.

Over the next few days I became aware of an undercurrent of excitement in the Castle. The little girls were all a-twitter, and they had a way of scattering upon discovery like mice at play. Illyrica spent hours in her room. When she was out in the public rooms she was never without some gorgeous tapestry in needlepoint, which she shoved away under various cushions, lap blankets, and dishes when certain people entered the room. Even Nora always seemed to glow. Childhood memories began to greet me at every turn, bringing with them a strange mix of melancholy and joy. The reason for all of this was simple enough. Christmas was just around the corner.

I had not thought much about my home since I had left it. But we had had Christmases there; glorious ones and bittersweet; and I thought of it now. I thought of my parents, long since gone from this world, of my childless aunt and uncle, whose was the title of the lands, and of my younger sister, who I barely knew. I thought equally as much of the horses in the old stables and the sea cliffs where I had often gone for long rides, letting the wild wind carry my soul up with it over the wintry sea. On my last Christmas at home, I had gone to the cliffs and spent much of my day there in dreaming, until the tips of my fingers and toes were in danger of frostbite despite the warm clothes I wore.

Dreaming of adventure. Of strange lands. And now here I was, in a strange land, surrounded by innocents and beauties of mysterious origin, and still no closer to any answer concerning them. I had been in the Castle since the summer, and I had begun to believe that I would leave it as ignorant as I had come. In any case, I would not be a hero here. That destiny awaited me with the Widow Brawnlyn. Of all the Castle's inhabitants, I fancied I might be of help to the Pixie alone. Nora had no need of me. The Giant seemed only to want to change me for his own purposes. I had grown tired of it.

Between my first visit to the Widow, when I routed the robbers from their forest den, and Christmas week, I had been back to the Brawnlyn House twice. Both times the Widow had given me work to do. Once she asked me for advice on how best to deal with a judicial matter; the second time, she sent me out to teach a notorious drunk a lesson. I did, and did it well. I saw more of Genevieve with each visit but knew her no better. The Pixie failed to escape the Castle on the first occasion, but on the second she accompanied me, and spent the whole of the day in the company of the noblewomen.

There was on the edge of the darkwood a hollow tree where the Widow took to sending messages for me. I checked it every day, often two or three times, and so it was that on the third day before Christmas I discovered an invitation, on fine ivory paper with a gilt edge, for the Pixie and I to attend a Christmas Eve ball at the Brawnlyn House.

The sun was setting as I passed through the cold woods to the Castle. The Pixie was in the front hall, helping direct a stream of little girls to the dining room, from whence came the smells of fresh-baked buns and a peculiar hot punch that only Nora could make. I pulled her aside and showed her the invitation. She flushed as she read it, and looked up at me with eyes so alive she almost took my breath away.

"We will go, Hawk?" she said. "We must!"

I frowned. "I will."

"You can't leave me behind!" she whispered. "You wouldn't. Lady Brawnlyn would never forgive you and you know it. *I* would never forgive you!"

I looked out at the hall and the last of the long-haired little beauties disappearing through the dining hall door. Illyrica was standing there. She cast a quizzical glance in our direction before following the cascade. Nora's voice could be heard over the chatter of the girls, giving directions.

"They'll expect you to be here," I said. "For Christmas Eve."

"As they will expect you," the Pixie said.

"That's different," I said. "You're part of the family."

The Pixie cocked her head a little. "So are you."

I didn't respond to the comment. "You can't just sneak out, Pixie. It won't work. You'd have to tell them."

The Pixie's demeanor grew quiet for a moment. She fingered the smoothness of the invitation in her hands.

"All right," she said. "I'll tell them." She began to move toward the dining room, then stopped and looked back. "The Angel may not let me go," she said.

I felt angry. "He cannot keep you," I said. "You're not a prisoner."

She shook her head, agreeing with me. "No," she said. Once more she looked down at the invitation, then resolutely tucked it away into a pocket in her skirt.

"Nora's made punch, and you know there's nothing else on earth like it," she said. "Are you going to stand there stupidly all night, or are you coming?"

I followed her into the dining room.

<hr />

On the second night before Christmas, the Giant came in from his vigil in the woods and joined us all in the soft room. He sat in his great chair, with children on his lap and shoulders and playing with his beard and his greying hair, while flames roared in the fireplaces and Nora read aloud from a storybook. The story was a romantic adventure in a magical, faraway land. I cast a glance at the Pixie now and then. She was sitting amidst the cushions near Nora, listening with a distracted entrancement that made me think she was writing her own story of nobility and far-off places. Illyrica sat near one of the fires, discreetly sewing and silently commanding any child who tried to peek at her work to pay attention to the story.

I sat in a corner of the room near Illyrica, looking neither at the Giant nor at Nora. If the Pixie made good on her threat, she would talk to the Giant tonight. I was not sure what I would do or say if they brought me into it—which I was nearly certain they would.

I must have looked as dark and gloomy as I felt, because I felt eyes on me. I looked up to find Illyrica watching me, her needle still, her head cocked in question. When she saw me looking at her she furrowed her brow, wordlessly asking what was wrong. I looked away.

Nora's even cadences picked up urgency as the hero of the story faced off with a terrible dragon. All around me, the girls leaned forward in breathless anticipation. The fire snapped and crackled.

And then it was over. The hero slew the dragon and rode away to his castle with the heroine. The whole room seemed to sigh with relief and stretch out languidly. The Giant spoke from his throne.

"Bed," he said. The children let up a wail of protest. The Giant smiled, gently taking a few down from his shoulders. "It is nearly Christmas," he told them. "Tomorrow night I shall see you again."

Isabelle spoke up. "We have made hundreds of paper chains for the Christmas Eve celebration," she said. "And Nora is making popped corn for us to string tomorrow."

The Giant smoothed back one of her curls. "I can hardly wait to see," he said.

Another little one piped up from the Giant's knee. "And Illyrica made something, but she won't show us yet."

Illyrica smiled at the little one, a beautiful, amused smile. The Giant looked gravely at the child. "I'm sure she will show us in her own good time," he said. "Now, to bed with you. All of you."

Obediently the children began to file out of the room, stopping on the way out to embrace some one or other of their elders. One seven year-old threw her arms around Nora's neck and asked, "Nora, what happened to the people in the story?"

"I'm sure they lived happily ever after," Nora answered.

"How do you know?" the little girl pressed.

Nora smiled. "They always do in stories," she said.

Satisfied, the little girl let go of Nora and ran after the end of the long-haired procession, legs pumping under her lacy pink nightgown.

The fire near me was beginning to die down. I picked up a poker and stirred it up again.

Nora looked up to a small ledge that surrounded the walls of the room. "I have been saving the candles we made last summer," she said. "Tomorrow night we'll bring them in and line them up all around the room and light them all at once. Do you remember, Pixie? You and I talked about it. You said it would look like a choir of angels had come into the room to hear the Christmas story with us."

The Pixie didn't meet Nora's eyes. She looked down and rubbed the back of her neck, drew a deep breath, and looked up at the Giant. "It will look beautiful," she said, "but I won't be here tomorrow night."

Every eye in the room turned to the Pixie in shock, save mine. I was still poking at the fire.

"What do you mean?" Nora asked.

The Pixie tossed her head. "There is a ball at the Brawnlyn House," she said. "Lady Brawnlyn has asked me to attend, and I am going."

Nora could hardly find words. "Lady—?"

"I've been there several times," the Pixie said. "Lady Brawnlyn and her daughter are very kind to me. They treat me like one of their own."

"But you *are* one of us," Nora said.

The Giant spoke for the first time. "It is better that you stay here," he said.

I felt my hackles rise. Lady Brawnlyn and Genevieve seemed to me just what the Pixie needed to grow past this place. She would look like royalty at the ball. Perhaps, after all, she was. What sort of life had the Giant prevented the Pixie from living? And why should he stubbornly continue to prevent her now?

All of a sudden there were eyes on me. Nora's eyes. "This has something to do with you, doesn't it?" she demanded. "Sparrowhawk, what have you done?"

I stood and turned to face her and the Giant. "I have introduced her to the nobles of the land… of *this* land. What is wrong with that?"

"We have no friendship with the outside world," the Giant said.

"*You* may not," I shot back. "I do. And so does the Pixie."

The Giant looked up at me. His eyes were full of quiet wrath. I was glad he was seated, for I was at eye-level with him. Had he towered over me, I did not know if I could have been so bold.

"You do not understand," he said.

"I understand that you are making this place into a prison," I answered. Nora's eyes blazed back at me, but she said nothing.

The Pixie looked at the floor, but she stood her ground. "Angel," she said, "I want to go."

The Giant stood without warning and left the room. His absence left the air full of unsettled emotion. Nora followed him without a word. Illyrica stood and made her way out a moment later, her needlework limp in her hand. There was no anger on her sensitive face, only sadness.

I replaced the poker by the fireplace and turned to the last remaining figure in the room. "Pixie—" I began.

She turned on her heel and left the room without a word.

No one spoke another word to me that night.

Chapter 16

————◆◆◆————

BROUGHT LOW

LIGHTS SHONE FROM EVERY WINDOW of Brawnlyn House as we approached it through the wintry night. It seemed an aristocratic beacon in the darkness: shining the light of luxury and costly extravagance over the shadowy landscape. The Pixie caught her breath at the sight of it, and I turned to look at her. She wore a fur-trimmed cloak of deep red over a simple dress of wood-pine green trimmed with lace. Nora had made the dress, and Illyrica the lace, and there was as much love in it as there was frost in the air. The dress made the Pixie's green eyes shine. She looked more like an innocent fairy fallen from some other, simpler world than she ever had before.

She looked at me, her eyes alight with the wonder of the house. "How can you look so dull?" she asked, with her old teasing smile made glorious by the rapture she felt. "Look at it! We're standing on the doorstep of heaven, Hawk."

She turned and tripped her way down the path toward the glowing house. I watched her go with the slightest of smiles. The unpleasant scene at the Castle was behind us now. The Pixie was right. Lit up as it was, Brawnlyn House looked like a celestial palace. Pride made me warm within. Through my own merits this place had become another home to me and to those who followed me.

They would be glad to see that we had come. The Pixie would be transformed—of course she could not wear the homespun dress to such an affair. Genevieve had promised to set aside one of her own gowns for her. The thought pleased me. I had for some time harboured a suspicion that the Pixie's descent was from some royal line. The Brawnlyns' treatment of her seemed almost to make this a fact; and tonight she would look every inch a queen.

Music greeted our ears as we approached the great doors. They stood open, spilling light and warmth out onto the stone drive and creating strange shadows in the gardens. I fell in step with the tune as I mounted the steps, and I smiled as the Pixie was spirited away from behind me by three of Genevieve's personal maids. She would not make her appearance at the ball until she was ready.

I swept my cloak from my shoulders and stepped boldly into the hall, head high, chest swollen. Handsome couples fell back from my approach in the whirl of the dance, and I heard the doorman announce my name: my real name, with all its accompanying titles. And to the end of it he attached this: "The Lord Hawk, captain of the realm!"

All around me the honourable lords and ladies of the surrounding lands danced, laughed, and spun conversation; ornate as moving paintings, elite like the wine that flowed freely. The Lady Brawnlyn herself stood most grand and imposing of all in a black dress of silk. Her eyes lit on me as I entered the room, and she called to me with a slight movement of her head. Carried along by the lights and the music, I reached her side quickly. A few friends had refrained from the dance to speak with her: she placed them in waiting as she turned to me and, in a low voice, acquainted me with those young men in the room who would certainly compete with me for Genevieve's attention in the festivities. I understood her well. She meant me to prevail in all such competitions.

"Acquit yourself well here," the Widow said. "You are among your own."

I bowed my head, smiling slightly. "Thank you, my lady."

She brushed close to me and said, in a voice lower still, "You shall not leave until the night is well spent, I hope. I have a matter of great importance to discuss with you."

"I will not leave until we have spoken to your satisfaction," I answered. She nodded and sent me away with a flick of her fan.

Genevieve was not just then in the room. I guessed, correctly, that she was with the Pixie. But she appeared within ten minutes, and her presence stirred the room. As ever, her face was unreadable. Her dark hair fell in gorgeous curls around her white neck and shoulders. She entered into the celebration with practiced ease, speaking but rarely, commanding attention nevertheless with her beauty and bearing. When she spoke it was in low tones; when she danced it was with perfect grace; when she turned her grey eyes on me, my heart nearly stopped with the feeling that in their depths was a lowering sky about to break.

I took her hand and led her into a waltz. As we danced I tried to talk with her.

"You look lovely," I told her as the room whirled past, but she did not respond. "Have you seen the Pixie?" I asked.

"I was with her a few moments ago," Genevieve answered.

"Is she coming?" I asked—feeling stupid, for the answer to that was obvious.

"Soon," Genevieve said, her lips curling up in what was almost a smile. "She is nearly presentable."

"I have promised to speak with your mother again tonight," I said. "I believe she has more work for me."

Genevieve laughed, a laugh that was without colour: grey and white and edged with bitterness. "Work for the Lord Hawk," she said. "I am sure you will prove yourself worthy yet again."

The music ended. She pulled away from me, turning to face the entrance of the ballroom. The Pixie had arrived.

I had once thought the Pixie too much a child to fall in love with. I knew that she was still. But dressed in the opulence of Genevieve Brawnlyn, with her hair entwined with gold and swept up off her neck, with every eye in the room fastened on her, the Pixie was the better of any grand lady in the room.

She looked like a queen.

Genevieve moved to greet her. The young men Lady Brawnlyn had pointed out to me also moved her way, but I was stricken and could not move. I had brought the Pixie into the eye of the world of the nobility, and something deep within me whispered that *I ought not to have done it.*

I shook the feeling off as best I could and tried to get to her, but I could not reach her in time. She was caught up in the dance, courted by the men, admired by the ladies: she was beautiful, glorious, at the height of her bewitching powers. When she laughed gaily it brought the whole room to her feet.

The night grew long. The attendants began to leave, one by one, two by two. I tried to keep up my attentions to Genevieve while fending off those with similar intentions, aware all the time that Lady Brawnlyn was watching me. I still felt guilty when I looked at the Pixie, and so I tried to ignore her. I drank wine and danced and compared stories with the men, and just as it struck me that I could not see the Pixie anywhere, Widow Brawnlyn beckoned me to her drawing room. I looked around wildly for the Pixie, torn between my need to answer the Widow's summons and my growing panic at my charge's absence. But the Widow was insistent. I withdrew to the drawing room to attend upon her in firelit solitude.

She looked up at me with greater solemnity than I had ever seen before. After the festitivites of the night, I was taken aback.

She wasted no time in getting to her subject. "It is late," she said. "I will spare you lengthy introductions. How much do you know about the place you currently call home, Hawk?"

"It is a pleasant haven," I said. "But secretive. I know its inner workings but little about its history."

"Sit down," the Widow said. I obliged.

"Not long ago, I became acquainted with a man whose story, in any other locality, would have seemed too wild to be believed," she told me. "Indeed, I was inclined to doubt him. But he introduced me to his whole family, and they echoed his report in every particular. I think it is true."

I shifted uncomfortably in my seat, wondering again where the Pixie had gone to. But the Widow's next words chased every thought of her from my mind.

"They told me that many years ago, while they were passing through this country on business, their middle child—a daughter—was stolen from them in the dead of night. They sought her out in vain, even spreading word that they would give every penny they owned for her return. Perhaps because of the family's relative poverty, the thief was not tempted. They never saw their child again. The nature of their business forced them to leave this land or starve, and ever since they have been trying to return. At last they have come back."

I closed my eyes. Desperately I tried to erase the image that came unbidden to mind—that of the Giant taking a child from her home and family. But it could not be.

"There is no need to look so stricken," the Widow said. "I am simply asking you to find the child if you can. I have reason to believe she may still be here in my lands."

"How am I to find her?" I asked. "There are hundreds—"

"Not hundreds like this one," the Widow said. "She should not be hard to recognize. The family, you see, had a specially strong attachment to her because she is afflicted—a mute, with a scar across her throat."

If I had not been seated, the sick feeling in my stomach might have knocked me off balance. I knew who she was describing.

Illyrica.

Had the mystery of the Castle's origins been solved for me by the Widow Brawnlyn? Could the Giant truly be a kidnapper—a thief, stealing children in the night as the rumours I'd once heard claimed?

I staggered out of the Widow's drawing room, having made no commitments nor uttered a word of my suspicions. I knew that if it was true—if Illyrica had been taken by force from her family—then I had to return her to them. No other choice could even be entertained.

The celebration was nearly over. I followed the directions of a few servants and took myself to the kitchens, where at last I found the Pixie. She was sitting on an old crate, her red cloak wrapped tightly around her, fingering an old sack. She looked up at me with the saddest smile I have ever seen.

"Look, Hawk," she said. "I found my royal seal."

I took the sack from her, hardly knowing what I was looking at. And then I saw it, stitched into the material: the words *R.S. Flour Co.* The lettering was just the same as in the Pixie's precious scrap of cloth.

She stood and dusted herself off, folding the sack. She was still wearing Genevieve's gown, but she had taken her hair down. She pulled her hood over it. "Let's go home," she said. "I'm tired."

We tramped through the snow and the darkness together, our thoughts holding us in separate worlds.

Finally the Pixie spoke. "I suppose there is some romance in being found in a flour sack," she said.

I mumbled my reply. "Not so much as in Illyrica's beginning."

"True," the Pixie said. "Kidnapping is very romantic."

She looked at me curiously, but I did not say another word.

Chapter 17

────◆◆◆────

ILLYRICA

IT WAS NOT A HAPPY CHRISTMAS. It almost seemed as though someone had died. The Pixie was moody and quiet. She took up her customary place among the daughters of the castle and led the celebrations dutifully, but all the heart had gone out of her. Both Nora and the Giant tried to act as though nothing was wrong, but I doubt that even the youngest child among us believed them. Once, for a moment, Nora let her guard down. She had just presented Isabelle with a beautiful handmade book of stories in Nora's own exquisite handwriting, and the child threw her arms around Nora's neck with the words, "I'll read it every night! I know it's full of happy endings!" I looked up at Nora's face and saw that she was about to cry. She regained control of herself, but I could not look at her again.

As for me: I was tormented. I could not look on the Giant. I avoided Nora. The Pixie avoided me. The children taunted me without trying to. I could not see a smiling, pink little face without picturing some bereaved mother weeping in the dark of the night; without picturing a family torn apart. Illyrica, silent, smiling, and ghostly as ever, conjured up horrible visions that I could not vanquish. And through it all I was nearly overpowered by what I tried to deny was guilt.

The gift-giving was not yet finished when I rose and left the room, looking behind me briefly. I felt, rather than saw, that the Giant watched me leave—still studiously avoiding him, I could not have seen his eyes on me. I fled the Castle and the wood. I fled to the Widow Brawnlyn.

She might have been expecting me, so little surprised was she to see me. I was admitted into her drawing room, breathless and flushed. "She is there," I said without preamble. "The kidnapped girl, the mute you told me about. She lives in the house in the darkwood north of here."

The Widow nodded. "Thank you, Hawk," she said. "What you are doing is right."

I closed my eyes against her condescending expression. Genevieve sat in a dark corner, taking in the exchange. I hoped—desperately—that she saw something heroic in my actions. I did not know what else to do. The man whose hospitality I had accepted all these months was nothing more than a villain, and I had to do what I could to restore Illyrica to her family. Yet I felt as if I had taken hands with the devil.

"Hawk!" the Widow said sharply. "Look at me."

I obeyed. Her face seemed softened, more understanding than it had ever been. "What you are doing is right," she repeated. "I can see that this is hard for you. But the girl's family had nearly given up hope. You have restored it."

I had restored it. I had given a destitute family hope. Slowly I felt some of my burden melt away. Yes. I had done what was right. I knew that I had to respond to the Widow, though words were beyond me. I nodded, feeling my spirit relax. "Thank you," I said.

Genevieve stood and abruptly left the room.

The Widow looked after her daughter with some displeasure. "Sit, Hawk," she said. "Have tea with me."

I shook my head. "No, my lady," I said. "If you please, it is Christmas. I should go... home."

"To the darkwood?" Widow Brawnlyn asked.

I hesitated. "Illyrica should be returned to her family," I said. "But... in many ways, the darkwood is a good home. Perhaps..." I turned away. I did not know what I meant or what I wanted to say. The Widow nodded as if she understood everything.

The sky was overcast. Dusk came early. I trudged back to the Castle, my footprints in the snow seeming deeper or lighter depending on my mood: lighter as I meditated on the Widow's reassurances, deeper as I thought of the place I was returning to.

Lights were bobbing in the Castle windows as I drew near. When I pushed open the heavy wooden doors, I was greeted by little girls in long nightgowns, holding small candles and bouncing eagerly on their toes. I smiled absently at them as they all chattered at me at once, something about a journey and looking for shelter. Then Nora's voice rose above them all. My weary eyes went to her face, and I was surprised to see compassion there. Her voice brought sense out of the babble.

"We do this every Christmas," she explained. "All together we journey through the house, knocking on every door. Looking for shelter, as the Christ child did long ago. And there is never a door opened to us. So all together we sleep in the soft room—"

"It is a stable," one of the children informed me.

"On the floor, and we remember what happened once in a stable." Nora looked down at the children and smiled. "Go," she said. "You have nearly knocked *down* every door in the Castle. It is time to go to sleep now."

The children filed out, still carefully clutching their candles, still excited.

"The candles?" I asked.

"They are carrying hope with them," Nora said. She drew a deep breath. "Hawk, if you are looking for shelter, you needn't stay out."

I cut her off. "I can sleep in my own room," I said.

"All right," she said.

I left the entryway and climbed the long stairs to my room. I was tired; confused. What would become of my report to the Widow I did not know. She had indicated that Illyrica's family were travellers. Perhaps they would not be found again, and nothing would change. Somehow it seemed probable.

I heard footsteps behind me and saw candlelight on the stone wall. I turned, ready to tell Nora that I was fine on my own. I don't know why I expected her to try and invite me to be with them a second time. But it wasn't Nora. Illyrica stood near me, holding out a gift wrapped in paper. Her blue eyes were deep and questioning. I dropped my head and reached out for the package.

It was soft beneath the paper. I sat down on the top step and slowly pulled away the ribbon that bound it. I pulled out a beautiful green piece of cloth, folded neatly in four. As I unfolded it, a scene came to life before my eyes. The darkwood was stitched in deep, glimmering colours, with the Castle in the center of it. Flying over it in a clear blue sky was a magnificent grey hawk. In its eyes was an expression of might and a protective spirit. The hawk was guarding the castle.

I looked back to the one who had created the little tapestry. She smiled at me. It was an odd, sad, knowing smile. I could not smile back.

"Thank you," I said at last, my tongue like lead.

She nodded once, slowly, and turned away. Her skirts swished around her as she gracefully descended the stairs, taking her candle with her, leaving me in the semi-darkness.

<hr />

I was awakened by a pounding at the door. Torchlight bounced on the walls as I descended the stairs, two and three at a time: ugly torchlight from outside the windows. A man's voice came muffled through the heavy wood.

"Open up in the name of the law!"

I recognized the voice. I had worked with the man on my hunts for criminals. He had always been subordinate to me.

Nora was already at the door, as was the Giant. Her back was against the wood. She was shaking her head as tears streaked down her face. But the Giant's hand was resolute. With deep eyes full of compassion he motioned her away and opened the door.

Six of the Widow's guards stood without. Behind them, in the murk of the starless night, there were others whose forms I did not recognize and whose faces I could not see.

"What do you want?" the Giant demanded. I saw the guards fall back a little as the Giant's bulk and evident anger confronted them. I had snatched up my cudgel on the way out of my bedroom door, and I tightened my grip on it now. I had fought alongside these men, but their manner now was one of enmity. I would fight them if I had to.

The guard in command cleared his throat and stepped forward. He held a long, ugly sword in his hand—unsheathed. "You have something here which does not belong to you," he said. "We demand that you give up the daughter of these good people at once."

The Giant narrowed his eyes as he peered into the darkness. "I see no good people," he growled.

One of the others who had been hiding behind the guards now stepped forward, a parchment in his hands, a horrible glimmer in his eyes. I recognized him at once. An iron weight pulled my heart down.

It was the cowardly gypsy we had once caught skulking in the woods.

He unrolled the parchment, torchlight glinting off the gold in his teeth. "You can see the proof all here," he said. "As if you don't remember... filthy thief."

The Giant took the parchment and examined it. Now and again his eyes flickered back to the armed guards, the torches, the waiting Gypsy. He cleared his throat and turned toward the hall.

"Illyrica," he called.

"No!" I heard the gasp escape from Nora, and saw the guards' swords come up in anticipation.

Illyrica appeared a moment later, softly closing the door of the room behind her—keeping the Pixie and all of the children from the guards' eyes. I could picture the scene before she had stepped out: I could see them clinging to her, pleading with her not to go. Yet she and the Giant seemed to understand. There was nothing they could do.

The gypsy grinned as Illyrica stepped into the torchlight. She looked at him steadily for a moment, and then turned to Nora. They clasped each other in their arms and kissed one another.

"Come on," the gypsy called. "We 'aven't got all night."

Illyrica stepped away and looked up at the Giant, her eyes speaking more gratitude and love than I had ever heard from the mouth of one who could speak. There was not a single mote of accusation. His eyes filled with tears as she stepped through the doors and into the hands of the shadowy people behind the guards, who clutched at her as if she would run away.

Would I had thrown myself in her path at that moment and beat the guards back myself. Would I had gone into prison or death to keep her from returning to *them*. But the sight of Illyrica's family, the knowledge of what I had done, had destroyed me. In that moment I could not have overcome a flea.

The Giant handed the parchment back to the Gypsy without a word. The evil little man sniffed, tucked the parchment away, and turned to go.

The guards stayed a little longer, waiting.

"Well," the chief of them said at last. "Aren't you going to close the doors?"

"No," the Giant said. "We are going to watch you leave."

Nervously, the guards nodded and turned away. Their torches bobbed across the lawns and faded into the darkwood. I stood in the doorway next to the Giant, while Nora cried behind us.

As soon as their torches had disappeared in the trees, the Pixie appeared, boots and coat already on, and took a step after them. The Giant put out a hand to stop her. She looked up at him with fiery eyes.

"They will harm her if we follow now," he said.

"They are—they are her family," I said. Even my tongue felt numb. I could hardly speak.

Nora did not look at me. "They maimed her once, Hawk," she said. "They would not hesitate to do it again."

The Giant looked down at us. "In a few hours, Pixie," he said. "In a few hours, you may follow them. Find out where they have gone."

Nora looked up, tears still running down her face. "We will go after her?" she said.

The Giant did not smile. His eyes were still on the woods. "Of course," he said.

Chapter 18

———— ◆•◆•◆ ————

THE PIXIE FINDS HELP

I DID NOT SLEEP THAT NIGHT.

When at last the Giant closed the doors, he turned and sat on the wooden chair outside of the soft room. He laid his head in his hands. Nora rubbed his shoulder, blinking back tears, until the Pixie drew her away. Arms around each other, they slipped through the door to the soft room. The Giant and I were alone. The entryway seemed terribly forlorn and barren. The Giant sat, motionless as a statue, and a lone torch flickered against the flag-stones on the floor and deepened the cracks between the stones in the walls.

I turned to trudge upstairs to my lonely room, but the Giant looked up just as my foot touched the first stair.

"Wait, Hawk," he said.

I turned.

"Stay on guard with me."

I opened my mouth to protest, but I could not argue with the command in his voice—no, nor with the way his eyes seemed more to implore than to command. I sat down across from the Giant and leaned against the wall, balancing my cudgel on my knees. I looked at the floor, and yet I could feel his eyes on me. A confession was trying to beat its way out of my heart, and I was doing everything in my power to hold it back. The pain was almost more than I could bear.

"The first night I saw you," the Giant said, "trying to fight your way into my woods, I saw courage and truth in your face. Where is it now?"

I swallowed. I neither looked up nor answered. I was not without words—but I did not want to give voice to them.

The Giant's voice dropped lower. "Tell me, Sparrowhawk," he said. "What have you done?"

Suddenly my mind was back in the darkwood of autumn, staff in my hand, sparring with the Giant in the night. It seemed that I heard him again, challenging me, offering me his hand, telling me to lay down my pride. Then, I had continued to resist him. I had thought it a virtue to keep from breaking at any cost. I had laid him low. But I could not do as much now. I sat in the presence of a great and mysterious man who I somehow knew to be full of righteousness' power, and I had done something terribly wrong. I was not yet sure how I had come to do it.

I saw suddenly that the only virtue left to me was that of relinquishment. I forced myself to meet his eyes. "I told her," I whispered. "I told the Widow that Illyrica was here. I think her spies must have followed me back."

I waited for the blow. The Giant had trusted me, allowed me access to the sanctuary he kept so protected, and I had opened its doors to the enemy. I waited now for him to crush me. But he did not. He said nothing. Was he waiting for me to continue? Now that I had looked at him, I could not look away. I was bound to speak whether I wanted to or not.

"She told me that Illyrica had been taken from her family, and I thought..."

"We took her to save her," the Giant said.

"I didn't know."

It seemed the worst of excuses. I *should* have known. I had seen the love and care that marked the inhabitants of the Castle. Why hadn't I known? For that matter, why had I been so quick to trust the Widow? All I knew of her was wealth and power and a title, and I had taken them as surety of character. All I knew of the Giant was character, and I had not trusted it because I did not understand him.

"I wish you had told me," I said, as all these things wrestled inside me. It was a weak thing to say: a word of blame, when the blame was all mine—and I knew it.

"You were not trustworthy then," the Giant said. "I wanted you to learn to see in the dark."

I tore my eyes away from him and looked at the flagstones. My eyes were beginning to fill with tears, but I was ashamed to cry. I was ashamed of everything.

"I think," the Giant said quietly, "that you are beginning to see now."

I almost looked up at him again. "I do not deserve your praise," I said.

There was a long silence. I could not see his face or the expression on it.

"You will," he said.

So deep was my bitterness, I hardly heard him.

The Pixie slipped out before dawn, a thick green scarf wrapped around her head, her hands covered in thin gloves. She knocked on every door in the town, and met with nothing but mistrust and animosity. For the first time she realized that what Nora had always said was true—there was no friendship between the Castle and the people of the town. They had been willing to treat the Pixie as the beautiful curiosity she was whenever she entered their streets, and she had often mistaken their desire to gossip and speculate for friendliness. Now she discovered that they regarded her, and the whole enterprise at the center of which her Angel reigned, with deep suspicion and even hostility. No one was willing to interfere in anything the Widow Brawnlyn might have done.

Hours passed. The Pixie turned almost in despair down the main street of the town. She had been turned away from nearly every door and venue. Head low, she bent into the wind as she passed by the tavern. Suddenly, she heard a sound she knew... and had not thought to hear for some months. A voice, and the plucking of strings. She stood in her tracks, and then flew at the tavern door.

A brute of a man appeared at the door and blocked her way.

"Let me in," she said, vexed almost to tears, trying her best to duck past him. His brawn seemed to fill up the whole doorframe. "Please get out of my way. There is someone inside I must see!"

"This is no place for a waif like you," the man said, stepping forward so that his presence pushed her nearly into the street. "Get off with you!"

Desperate, the Pixie stood on her tiptoes for a better look into the tavern. Catching sight of the man she wanted, she waved her arms and shouted.

"Here now, none of that!" the big man said, and he might have thrown her out bodily if there hadn't been an answering shout from the tavern.

"By heavens!" the voice said. "Pixie, is that you?"

In answer, the Pixie dissolved into tears. She stood in the street, crying and wiping at her eyes and nose with her coat sleeve, as the Poet asked leave to pass by the brute in the doorway and made his way out to her, lute in hand. She look at him with glistening eyes and nodded an answer to his question.

"Oh, dear," the Poet said, groping about his person for a handkerchief. "Dear child, what can have happened? Surely you are all right?"

To this, the Pixie could only shake her head. She grabbed at his sleeve and began to pull him down the street. "Come with me," she said. "I'll explain everything, only come with me…"

The Poet followed along, but stopped after a few steps. "Now, this isn't quite regular," he said. "Do tell me, Pixie, what is wrong? Nothing has happened to the Giant?"

"No," the Pixie managed to say. "No, it is not the Giant. Oh, Poet, our own good Poet, it's Illyrica… she's been taken away by the most horrid men, and we cannot find out where they've taken her, and no one will help me…"

While she was speaking, the Poet went pale. The Pixie told me that a white fire seemed to light in his eyes, and for a moment she was frightened of him. Never before had the Poet, so awkward and verbose, looked so handsome or been so silent. When he spoke again, there was an entirely new note of strength in his voice.

"I knew I had come back here for a reason," he said. "Now tell me everything."

Out there on the street, the Pixie told the Poet all she knew. And she told him that it was essential that they learn where the awful little gypsy and his "family" had gone, but the townspeople would not breathe a word to her.

"Calm down," he said. "Calm down, child. Here… hold my lute." She took it. Without another word he turned and re-entered the tavern.

The Pixie was never quite sure what happened next. She knew that the Poet was gone for a good long time. She stood in the street cradling the lute for an hour and a half at least, and then suddenly a great smashing and yelling kicked up inside the tavern. She nearly rushed in to save the Poet from certain humiliation and death, but in a rare moment of wisdom she realized that involving herself might make things harder on him. Minutes later, the big brute appeared at the door with another man of like size, and together they threw a tousled and bloody-nosed Poet into the street. He picked himself off the cobblestones, shook his white-knuckled fist at the door, and bellowed, "Base, worthless cowards! May your soup always be cold, and may you never be taken for gentlemen!"

He turned and took his lute gently from the Pixie's arms. She was, she told us, scarcely breathing for desire to know whether the Poet had been successful. When he pointed down the road to the west her heart nearly skipped a beat.

"They have gone in a caravan to the west," he said. "They left early this morning, and cannot be moving fast, for they have several wagons. The drunken poltroons within estimate that a good man on horseback could catch up to them in an hour or two."

"We do not have horses," the Pixie said. She bit her lip. "It doesn't matter. The Angel will know what to do."

And so it was that the Pixie returned to the Castle with the Poet in tow, looking as though he had recently been dragged by the ankles through a barnyard. She told us the story quickly, her cheeks flushed and her eyes angry as she told us of the town's reception. Her eyes filled with tears again as she said, "They're afraid—of the Angel! And the cowards would let those monsters get away with Illyrica..."

"Hush, Pixie," Nora said. She began to unwind the scarf from the Pixie's neck. "We will not let them get away, no matter what the villagers do."

"But it's all right," the Pixie said. "The Poet found them."

The Giant spoke for the first time, from his seat near the iron stove.

"Where are they?" he asked.

Chapter 19

———◆———

A LONG NIGHT'S WAIT

THE POET RELAYED HIS INFORMATION quickly. The Giant stood. His presence dwarfed my spirit as much as it did my body. But for the first time, I felt no challenge in his strength. I was cowed, but I was also comforted; and I waited for him to speak, even as he pulled on his boots and reached for the fur greatcoat he wore in the woods at night.

"You must follow them," the Giant said, looking first at me, then at the Poet. "Both of you. Hitch up the pony and drive her as hard as you can. The carnival—yes, it is a carnival she travels with—will make camp for the night. You will catch up to them then, if not before. Listen to me carefully. These people do not care about Illyrica. They are greedy and full of themselves. They came here last night to prove that their power is greater than mine, and for no other reason. Don't provoke them. I am sending you to be sure Illyrica is safe. Do not give them reason to lash out against her."

The Poet and I looked at one another and nodded. The Giant continued. "I will come after you," he said. "Wait for me. Keep your eye on her; make sure she is safe. If she is not, you will know what to do."

Here I nearly protested. I had already destroyed so much

by my foolish decisions. More than anything I wanted to make myself right through all of this, but I could not trust myself to do it. The Giant stopped me from speaking when he looked into the Poet's eyes.

"Do what you must, because you love her," the Giant said. He almost smiled at the look on the Poet's face. "Yes," the Giant said. "I do believe that you do. It is about time we met face to face, you and I. From now on you are welcome here, always."

He turned to me and laid his great hand on my shoulder. His stern, dark-browed face looked down on me. "Do it, Hawk, because it is right."

I nodded.

"Let me go, too." The three of us turned as one. Nora had stood, and her eyes were fixed on the Giant. "Please, Angel," she said.

He frowned. "The Castle needs you."

"The Pixie can take care of things here," Nora said. "Please."

The Giant looked away. "I do not want you in danger."

"What if Illyrica is hurt?" Nora asked. Her voice quavered, whether at the thought of her friend's danger or because she was challenging the Giant, I did not know. "They cannot help her as I can. I have nursed her through injury before. Angel, she will need me."

I thought I knew what thought lay unspoken beneath Nora's words. She had to be there. She had to see it all for herself. If something went wrong and we did not return with Illyrica—somehow I knew that Nora could not bear to hear about it from a distance. Whatever horrors might await us, she would rather live through them than by haunted by imagination.

Finally the Giant nodded. "You are right," he said. "You may go."

The Pixie stirred. I thought she was about to ask permission to come as well. The Giant turned his compassionate eyes on her. She was still flushed. Emotion lay behind her eyes like a ceaselessly disturbed well.

"Take care of the children," was all he said to her. With that, he stalked out of the kitchen. "Hawk!" he called over his shoulder.

I looked at my travelling companions before stepping out after him. "I will hitch up the wagon," Nora said. "Poet, the Pixie will help you pack us something to eat."

I followed the Giant out onto the snowy lawns. He waited until we had walked a good way from the house and turned to me. "Take care of Nora also," he said. "She loves very deeply and is very easily hurt."

"I will do my best," I said.

"I will come as soon as I can," the Giant said. "It will be hard to wait, but you must do so if you possibly can."

One final time he laid his hand on my shoulder. His eyes searched out my soul. He nodded, as if satisfied with what he had found there, turned, and walked away into the woods. I watched him go before I turned back to the Castle.

⊷◆⊶

We found the caravan by midday. They were traveling slowly, almost luxuriously. We left the pony and the cart by a stream and followed the villains on foot, keeping far enough back that they would not detect our presence. We could only trust that Illyrica was with them, and safe for the moment. There was no way we could get close enough to them now to know for sure. We followed in silence, each of us lost in our own thoughts, and yet entirely unified—more dedicated to one another than ever human beings have been, for the common cause we shared.

Toward evening, the caravan at last came to a halt. Men and women of evil exterior crawled down from several wagons and began to set up camp. The carnival consisted of four or five garishly painted wagons, smeared with dirt and extra paint, and a few other carts containing cages and strange contraptions. In the cages were exotic beasts, ill-favoured and badly cared for. A few mangy yellow curs ambled and fought around the wagon wheels, shying away from curses and kicks whenever a human came near.

"I shall go into the camp," the Poet said. I reached out and laid my hand on his sleeve, meaning to prevent him.

"Should we not wait until they are asleep?" I asked.

"No," he said. "They don't know me. I am but a wandering minstrel, a performer as they are. At worst they will turn me away. I do not want to wait any longer to find her."

"Go," Nora said. "Go, and tell us what you find."

I was not happy about splitting up, but I nodded. The Poet crept out of the bushes and stood up straight in the road, brushing himself off and flicking bits of dirt and bark out of his hair. He still bore the marks of his fight at the tavern. One of his sleeves was torn and the collar of his winter vest was bloody. He slung his lute carefully over his back and headed into the camp. The yellow dogs greeted him with howls and snarling. He sidestepped them very bravely and greeted the little Gypsy who had come out to meet him. The sight of the man filled me with anger. When I had seen his face that first night in the woods, I had not imagined how much grief and harm he intended to bring on us. I could almost wish I had killed him—but no. Somehow it was right that I had not, just as it was right that I was here to face him again if need be.

The wagons had been pulled into a circle. The Poet disappeared on the other side of them. We could hear voices, but could discern neither words nor tone. Nora had been crouching beside me in the bushes at the side of the road, but now she moved back with a sigh.

"We may as well make camp ourselves," she said. "The Angel will not be here until tomorrow night, and heaven knows when the Poet will return to us."

She was right. I followed her farther from the road, into a nearby hollow where the light of our fire would not likely be seen by the carnival. Nora began to gather sticks for a fire immediately. I moved quickly alongside her.

"Let me," I said.

"Please, Hawk," she said. "If I don't keep busy I will go mad."

I nodded and stepped back. "I will build the fire."

"The sun will not set for another two hours at least," she answered. "We shouldn't waste fuel."

"Then tell me what I <i>can</i> do!" I burst out. I looked down at my hands. I had no right.

She stopped, straightened, and looked up at me, her arms full of sticks. "I'm sorry," she said after a moment.

I shook my head. "No," I said. "I don't really know why the Giant sent me on this mission."

"He sent you because he believes in you," Nora said. There was a large stone in the center of the hollow. She sat down on it slowly, lowering the sticks onto the ground. I didn't know how to interpret the look in her eyes as she regarded me. When I had first come to the Castle she had treated me with thiny veiled hostility. Over time, that had given way to silent acceptance. Now she seemed to look on me with strange compassion, and I did not know why. Had I not done more than anyone else living to break up the home she loved? But then, perhaps she did not know what I had done.

I lowered myself down on the ground across from her, avoiding her gaze. "He has chosen you, Hawk," she said. "And I… I know that he does not make his decisions lightly. I have not been a friend to you since you came to the Castle. I'm sorry."

An apology was the last thing I expected from her. I looked up at her, taken aback by the genuine sorrow in her blue eyes; by the tentative friendliness. I did not know what to say.

"You have nothing to be sorry for," I answered at last. "I have only brought grief to you."

Nora shook her head. She had tied her golden hair back in a bun earlier that day, and strands of it were coming loose now. She brushed a long strand back. "If I had trusted the Angel as I should have, perhaps you would have trusted him more easily yourself. I should have welcomed you."

"You should be angry with me," I said.

She smiled sadly. "When so much is at stake," she said, her eyes turned toward the carnival, "only a fool takes the time to be angry."

"You sound like the Giant," I told her.

"I ought to," she said. "I have been with him long enough."

I had never expected to hear the mystery of the Castle explained simply—certainly not from Nora. From the first day I heard of the Castle, I had given my imagination free reign. As I had fallen under the spell of the Widow's influence, my wonderings turned to doubt and the fair mystery became black and dreadful. But Nora was determined now that she would trust me as the Giant did. She told me the story.

"My father was a fisherman in a country east of here," she said. "The Angel was a blacksmith in the village where my parents lived. He was my father's oldest and dearest friend. Many nights he would come and sit by our fire. He frightened me then, with his great dark face and his hands always black with soot. I can still remember looking up at him from my mother's knee, though I was only a tiny child then... no more than three."

Nora looked down at her hands. She held a twig and rubbed her fingers up and down its smooth bark.

"It was the same year that plague struck our village. It killed both my parents. Before he died, my father asked the Angel to care for me. He promised that he would. He carried me away from the village that same night. I rode in a sling on his shoulder, and clung to him for days. We journeyed together until the Angel found the Castle in ruins. He spent years fixing it up, making it livable again, and roaming the woods for our food and livelihood—even then, the Angel sold furs so that we could eat through the winter.

"When I was six, the Angel and I went to the border of the province, selling furs. We came across a ruined caravan. We could not tell who they had been—the wagons had burned to ashes. The passengers had all been killed by robbers. All except one. A little way off the road we found a baby, playing with an old bit of cloth."

"The Pixie," I said.

"Yes," Nora answered. She smiled, and her eyes shone as she spoke. "She was the most beautiful child. I thought I had gone to heaven when the Angel said she could come and live with us. A few years later, we began to take in others. Some were orphaned by plague, others by fire or thievery. Isabelle's parents brought her to us. They had heard that there was a haven in the darkwood for abandoned children, and they asked us to take her, for they were starving. They said they would come back for her in a year or two, but they never returned."

"And Illyrica?" I asked.

Nora's face clouded over. "Illyrica was the only child we ever took from an unwilling family… if they *are* her family. They have papers to say so, although I believe her parents are dead. It was only seven years ago—Illyrica was eleven. The Pixie snuck out of the Castle one day. A carnival had come to the town, and she wanted to see it. When she came back she told us that there was a beautiful little girl there who could not speak, and she always looked frightened. She said the carnival owners kicked her and called her names, and made her feed the half-wild animals though she was terrified of them. It upset the Pixie so much she could hardly tell us about it. The Angel went out the same night and tried to convince Illyrica's family to let her come with us. They would not give her up. They are cruel people, unimaginably cruel… in some shows they would do dreadful things to her, because it entertained the crowd that she would not scream. We don't believe it was an accident that her vocal chords were cut."

I closed my eyes. The whole story was horrible. Nora's voice was taut, and it trembled slightly as she spoke. "Before they left town, the Angel went to them one last time. While he kept them busy, the Pixie and I snuck into their tents and stole Illyrica away with us."

She fell silent. I looked up at her. She was looking off toward the caravan again. "I hope the Poet is all right," she said.

It grew dark, and I lit the fuel Nora had gathered. The air was cold. We sat near the fire, wrapped in our cloaks, and once Nora wordlessly passed me a small loaf of bread. I could not eat.

From the wagons came the sounds of coarse laughter and music, and I thought I heard the plunking sound of the Poet's lute. At least they seemed to be on friendly terms. I stared into the fire, trying not to imagine in too much detail what the camp was like at that moment, or where Illyrica might be. When I looked over at Nora, I saw that she had pulled her knees to her chest and sat with her head bowed on them, eyes closed. Whether she was sleeping I could not tell, and did not ask.

A sudden crashing in the trees startled us both. Nora lifted her head. I was on my feet, sword in hand. The Poet's voice came through the trees, and we both relaxed.

"Oh dear," he was saying. "Dear, dear..." He burst into our little clearing, flustered and grimy with smoke. I could smell alcohol hanging about his clothes, though he did not seem drunk. He mopped his brow with relief as he took in the sight of us. "I feared I would not find you," he said. "They have let me go for the moment... I told them I needed to, er, relieve myself. They are most insistent, most demanding! And they have no taste in fine music. The ballads they want to hear!"

"Is Illyrica all right?" Nora asked.

The Poet nodded. I saw pain in his expression and wanted to look away. "They are not kind to her," he said, "but they have done no real harm."

"Did she see you?" I asked.

"Yes," he said. "I have never seen eyes so full of hope." He was crying. I bowed my head. I had been ashamed to cry for my own sins, but I knew that there was nothing shameful in this man's tears of love.

"Where is she?" Nora pressed.

The Poet nodded in the direction of the camp, mopping again at his forehead with a handkerchief that had once been white. "The yellow wagon," he said. "It is full of props and costumes. She sleeps there. They let her out only when they have work for her to do."

Nora nodded, looking away to hide the pain in her own eyes.

⊸◈⊶

The Poet returned to the camp, and the fire died down to embers. I stayed half-awake, half-asleep; awake just enough to keep the fire from going out. Sometime late in the night I heard a sound that brought me fully to my senses. Someone was moving in the camp.

Slowly, silently, I opened my eyes and rolled over so that I could spring to my feet at a moment's notice. I looked around me. Nora was gone.

I arose just in time to see Nora slipping away through the trees, wrapped in her cloak. I followed on silent feet. The Giant had taught me to move through the forest as quietly as an owl in flight, and my feet fell into the old familiar patterns now. If Nora knew I was behind her, she did not show it.

I followed her through the woods to the camp. The wagons stood now in eerie silence, broken by the muffled sounds of snoring and animals moving. Nearest to us was the yellow wagon, its paint chipped and grimy. In the moonlight its colour was sickly.

Nora crept up to the side of the wagon and ran her hands over it, looking for some kind of door. I hung back, keeping to the trees, moving just enough that I could keep Nora in my sight. She circled the end of the wagon, and I swung myself up into a tree branch to get a better view.

From where I was now, I could see that a sliding door on the other side of the wagon had been left open. It gaped big and black in the night. Below it, on the ground, a shadowy figure rested with one arm on the wagon floor and her head resting in the crook of her elbow. Nora stood still for a moment when she saw the figure, and then stepped forward carefully, laying her hand on Illyrica's shoulder. I saw Illyrica awake and raise her head. Nora knelt beside her and slipped her arms around her. I wondered for a moment why they did not run for the woods, and then I saw by the way Illyrica sat that she was not entirely free to move. I guessed that her arm was tied or chained to something in the wagon.

Nora pulled her cloak off her shoulders and wrapped it around Illyrica. I wondered if I heard her whispering, or if it was only my imagination.

They remained together until dawn. I spent the night shivering in the tree branches. Our fire, long since dead, tantalized my imagination. But I had seen Nora give her cloak away and knew that she, too, was cold—and somehow I could not complain, not even in my own thoughts. Just as light began to streak the sky, I climbed down from the tree and stretched my stiff and aching muscles. Keeping a wary eye open for dogs, I crossed the clearing to the wagon. Nora and Illyrica were both asleep, leaning on each other. Somehow they had contrived to share the cloak between them. I could see now that Illyrica was indeed held to the wagon, by a short chain attached to a post on the inside.

I hissed Nora's name. She opened her eyes and looked at me almost immediately. Without a word she rose, tucked the cloak firmly around Illyrica, and followed me out of the camp.

When we reached the ashes of our dead fire, I said, "The Angel *will* free her."

"He will," Nora said. "Or I will take her place."

She added the last words so quietly that for a moment I wondered if I had imagined them. I knew I had not. Nora had come to rescue Illyrica, and nothing would stand in her way.

Chapter 20

———◆———

THE ANGEL
STRIKES A BARGAIN

THE MORNING WAS COLD and incredibly clear. I was afraid that the caravan would pack up and move on, taking us farther away from the Giant, but the occupants of the wagons were hung-over and disinclined to travel. This, and a torrent of oaths and curses accompanied by the howls of the dogs, alerted me and most of the camp to a problem with the front axle on one of the wagons. The Poet was still with the carnival people somewhere, sleeping in or under a wagon. Nora and I, wide awake, found ourselves places in the surrounding woods from which we could watch the camp and hear most of what was going on.

Illyrica appeared before long, carrying a load of wood on her back. She put it down in the center of the camp and began to build a fire. Her hands and head were bare, and I imagined that her fingers were nearly numb as she worked to get the fire going. At last a tendril of smoke appeared, and a tongue of flame licked its way up from the wood. The evil little gypsy stepped up beside Illyrica and shoved her away.

"Keep out of my way, brat," he muttered, holding his gloved hands over the fire to warm them.

The fire attracted other denizens of the camp. Before long many of them had left their wagons and stepped into the light of day. There were twelve or so. The little Gypsy appeared to be the leader, seconded by an aging woman whose face was hard and cruel. They were a rag-tag bunch, all of them dirty, unkempt, and miserable in their ways. There were no children among them. The youngest of the band was a long-haired boy of about seventeen.

They were as indolent as they were dirty, and though Nora and I did not move from our posts for the better part of the day, not one of them did anything worth noting. The Poet sat outside one of the wagons, looking as though he did not know what to do with himself. The people of the caravan ignored him, apparently too thick with laziness to care that he was among them. Illyrica carefully kept her distance from him. He was careful not to watch her too obviously, but more than once I saw them exchange glances. His presence in the camp was a silent promise to Illyrica that she would not be abandoned.

The old woman brought out a kettle full of some vile porridge. Calling them all by various and unfriendly names, she poured out a bowl for each of her travelling companions. The Poet was given a bowl, which he choked down with the best will he could muster. Illyrica was ignored.

The day wore on. The Giant might arrive at any time. Though he had promised to be there by sundown, I knew that he would have given himself extra time. Perhaps, after all, he would not need it. But he did not come. The gypsy and a hulking young man of indeterminate age went to work on the axle, swearing and complaining, and doing a poor job of it. Noon arrived, and once again the old woman brought out food. It was better fare this time: bread, meat, cheese, and a great deal of drink. Nora crept back to our own encampment and returned to me with a loaf of bread and dried venison. Once again, Illyrica was given nothing. Desperately I wished that she would come near us so that we could give her of our own lunch, but she did not go beyond the wagons. She had been with them all the day before, and I wondered if she had eaten anything since leaving the castle.

When they had eaten their fill, the carnival people called to the Poet to give them some music. While he played, they continued to drink. As the day wore on, I grew increasingly nervous. If the Giant hoped to reason with these people, he was likely to be disappointed. The sky began to darken. Still the Poet kept the villains entertained; still Illyrica moved only when she was commanded by the old woman to fetch something and cursed for her trouble. There was no sign of the Giant.

By the time the sky had grown well and truly dark, the Poet seemed ready to collapse with exhaustion. He finished a country ballad to raucous laughter and applause from the group, and then the Gypsy stood and began to decant, telling stories of the carnival's journeys across many a province, and of the wild shows with which they did their own share of entertaining. He punctuated his tales with calls for food and drink, which the old woman produced with the help of Illyrica. Once I saw the Poet make a move to offer his meat to her, but the old woman pushed her beyond the circle before he could manage it.

Nora grabbed my arm suddenly. "Hawk," she said.

I looked where she was pointing. Illyrica had come around one of the wagons and was leaning against it with her eyes closed, faint with hunger. The smell of food and wine was strong in the air, and I could only imagine how weak it made her feel. But it was not Illyrica's hunger that alarmed Nora. The hulking young man who had worked on the axle was also coming around the end of the wagon.

Illyrica opened her eyes just in time to see him. She started back. He held out a hunk of bread. "Take it," he said. "I know you're hungry."

Hesitantly, Illyrica stepped forward and reached for the bread. Before she could react, he grabbed her wrist with his other hand. The glint in his eye made me sick to my stomach.

"Well, look at you, brat," he said in a low voice. "Haven't you grown?"

Where she found the strength I don't know, but Illyrica wrenched her arm free. She ran. Nora's grip on me tightened as I tensed to follow. "Not yet," she said. We watched as Illyrica stumbled into the circle by the fire.

The gypsy was in high dudgeon, a bottle of wine in one hand as he told his stories. Illyrica's sudden entry into the firelight knocked the bottle from his hand. He hardly missed a beat. He grabbed hold of Illyrica's arm and shoved her forward, where everyone could see her.

"Now *here's* a story!" the gypsy cried, slurring his words. "After all these years she comes back to us! And we'll use her right well, won't we, eh?"

He moved too quickly—we didn't see it coming. Before anyone could move, the gypsy had taken up a cane. "We'll teach you!" he cried, his face purple with wine and sudden anger. "Don't you *never* run away again!" He brought the cane down across Illyrica's neck and shoulders. The crack resounded in the clearing. She gasped with pain and fell to her knees.

The gypsy raised the cane once more, but before he could bring it down, the Poet's hands were at his throat. The Poet was in a hot rage, his lute flung away, his eyes blazing. I could hear the gypsy gagging as the Poet bore him to the ground, fists and feet flailing.

Everything happened so fast that I cannot be sure how any of us ended up where we did. Several of the ruffians reached for the Poet, but I was at his side in an instant, and I fought them all back at once. The old woman apparently decided that Illyrica had not been punished enough. She snatched up the cane and raised it to strike, but before she could, Nora had wrenched it from her hands and dealt her two strong blows with it.

There were only four of us, and the fight turned against us quickly. I ceased to fight when I felt a knife at my throat. The teenage member of the carnival had half climbed up on my back, and held me captive. Two others dragged the Poet off of the Gypsy, and from the corner of my eye I saw the hulking young man bearing down on Nora and Illyrica. He pulled the cane away and threw Nora to the ground.

"Stop!" I heard myself shouting. "Stop it, all of you!"

For some reason, they listened. The gypsy appeared before me, sweating and breathing hard. He snarled at me as he approached and slapped me across the face.

"Why should we listen to you?" he growled. "Who are you to give orders in *my* camp? I know you, you traitorous little whelp!"

"Let them go," I said, nodding toward Illyrica and Nora. "You have no right to keep them here."

"The girl is *mine*," the gypsy hissed. "My own brother's girl. I have papers to say that she belongs to me, and I'll do whatever I like with her."

The Poet spoke this time, trembling with rage between the men who held him. "Do not touch her again!" he said. "I will not allow it!"

The Gypsy glared at him and turned back to me. "It seems," he said, "that you are all in a nasty way of pretendin'. You are not the victors here. That's me."

"What do you intend to do with us?" I asked.

In answer, he half-turned and held out his hand. The young man handed him the cane. He slapped it against his hand, just to hear the sound of it. "What sounds good to me," he said, "is I'll beat you all within an inch of your lives and leave you and your flunkies out in the road to crawl home on your bloody 'ands and knees!" He grinned, the gold in his teeth flashing in the firelight. "And just to make it interesting, I'll start with that runaway girl of mine. Just to prove to you who's lord in this camp!"

He jerked his arm, loosening it up, and turned. "Bring her here," he said.

The young man reached down and pulled Illyrica up by the arm. I could see the red streaks of blood on her neck.

"What is she worth to you?" I demanded.

The gypsy turned back to me. "What's that?" he asked.

"What is she worth to you?" I repeated. "She's only a girl, not strong, not even whole. I can give you better."

"What can you give me?" the gypsy asked, leaning in closer. His breath reeked. I set my jaw to keep from wincing.

"Myself," I said. "I'll stay. I'll sign papers; keep me for a bond-slave. But let her go, and the others."

The gypsy appeared to consider it for a minute. But then his upper lip curled. He turned back to Illyrica, raising the cane.

"What is she worth to you?" I cried again. I strained against the arms that held me, heedless of the knife that still pressed against my throat.

A deep voice, from somewhere outside the light of the camp-fire, boomed out in the night. "Answer the question."

I turned. We all did. A massive shadow stood between the wagons, arms folded. I closed my eyes in a moment of relief. The Giant had come. He was only one man, but the force of his presence was undeniable. The people of the caravan stepped back. Nora reached down and took Illyrica's hand, pulling her to her feet beside her.

The Giant stepped into the light of the fire. Dressed in bearskin and heavy fur, he looked like a wild and ancient spirit of the woods. His face was magnificent to behold. Towering over the base creatures of the carnival both in spirit and in power, he had never looked more like a legendary giant—nor had he ever looked more like an angel.

The boy who held me captive loosened his hold and made to step away, but the gypsy saw him and held up his hand to stop him. "Hold the prisoners!" he commanded. He was still drunk, and the drink made him bold. He stepped closer to the Giant, dwarfed in every way, and looked up at him with a yellow-eyed sneer.

"You're on my territory now," he said. "You saw the papers; you know my rights."

The Giant glared down at him. "You have no right to hold my friends," he said. "Let them go."

Cowed a little by the power of the Giant's voice, the gypsy backed away and nodded to his cohorts. "Let go of them."

The knife at my throat was pulled away. I stepped to the Giant's side. The Poet and Nora joined me—but Illyrica was still with them, still one of them by every legal tie. She looked at us with a sweet sorrow in her eyes, and desperation built like bile in my throat. We could not leave her—not if it meant breaking every law in the land.

"You have not told me," the Giant said. "What is the girl worth to you?"

The gypsy was still backing away. He stopped when he reached Illyrica and stepped half in front her. "She's not for sale," he said. "You think you can come here and take what you want just because you're bigger than we are. Well, you're not bigger than the law."

The Giant nodded at me. "This man offered you his life for her," he said.

The gypsy sneered. "I don't want him."

The Giant reached into his coat and pulled out a heavy bag. Even in his hands it looked large, and it jingled when it moved with the unmistakable sound of coins. He weighed it in his hand a moment and threw it at the Gypsy. The little man scrambled to catch it. The weight of it nearly pulled him down to the ground. Struggling to hold it, he opened the bag. His eyes grew wide. The firelight glinted off the contents. We all saw it.

It was gold.

There was a small fortune in that bag—more than I had ever seen. I heard Nora gasp, and the ruffians murmured together. I looked up at the Giant, my eyes wide.

The gypsy was obviously battling within himself. Never again would he see so much money, yet taking it meant bowing to the Giant's will. Pride and greed shone in his face, twisting his features so that they were even more hideous than before.

He looked up at the Giant and licked his lips. "You would buy her for this?" he said.

The Giant lowered his dark brows. "I would not buy any human being," he said. "But I will buy the papers that give you a right to her."

The gypsy looked back down at the money. He ran his fingers through the coins, muttering to himself. And then he waved his other hand in the air. "The papers," he said. "Give him the papers."

Someone scurried off and returned with the papers. The Giant took them, and with great care tore them to shreds. He looked up, frowning. Illyrica was still held, by the hulking young man and the old woman.

"Release her," the Giant said.

The gypsy nodded, and the scoundrels let her go. Almost unbelieving, Illyrica rubbed her arms and moved forward, looking to every side as though someone would prevent her at any moment.

As she moved past him, a strange rage overtook the Gypsy. He reached out to stop her, swinging her around to look at him. "Devil take you!" he swore, and swung the cane at her.

The Giant caught it. He ripped it out of the gypsy's hands and struck him one heavy blow. The gypsy screamed and clutched the bag of money to him. The Giant stopped abruptly and broke the cane in two. He threw it away and looked down on the gypsy without saying a word. Then, with a sad shake of his head, he turned to Illyrica. She reached out for him with both hands and ran forward. He caught her up and nestled her head against his chest. Exhausted, she fainted in his arms.

I looked over at Nora. She was smiling, her eyes alight with tears. Illyrica was safe. The Giant had worked a miracle.

Chapter 21

CHANGES

WHETHER IT WAS THE ABUSE she had suffered or the hopelessness of staring into a future without love that affected her most, no one could be sure—but Illyrica was not quick to recover. Life around the Castle was hushed and solemn for days after we returned. The Giant carried her up the stone steps to her room high in the west turret, and there in her bed she lay for days, never entirely waking. She was never alone. The Poet sat with her often, at the end of the bed, leaning forward with his chin on his hands. His lute was draped across his back, always silent. His eyes were worried and his manner distracted. There was no music in his heart now… there could not be until Illyrica awoke.

Nora was by Illyrica's side whenever her work around the Castle would allow, which was often. I saw to it that most of the outdoor work was done, and that there was always water and firewood in the kitchen. The Pixie had not done a marvelous job of housekeeping while we were away—I did not blame her, for I could see along with everyone else how tormented she was over the whole affair. She avoided me as much as she had immediately after the Christmas ball, but I kept myself too busy to notice overmuch. Even so, Nora seemed content to let household matters alone more than usual. She delegated much of the work to the Pixie and Isabelle, and sat by Illyrica's side, reading to her though she did not respond.

The Giant was away from the Castle almost perpetually. He seemed to have increased his vigil in the woods. Yet, every night I would hear him enter the house, and I knew that he was going to stand over Illyrica's bed and look down on her with his dark eyes—to wrap her somehow in his heart and will her to wake.

I met the Poet one day as he marched down the stairs. He had been so little away from Illyrica's side that his appearance alarmed me.

"No, no," he said when I asked him if something was wrong. "I think… I hope… she will awake soon."

Without another word he continued down the stairs and out of the Castle, to return two hours later with a trio of unplucked chickens slung over his shoulder. He tramped into the kitchen and sat down on a low stool, his long legs angling out awkwardly, and attacked the chickens with a vengeance. Feathers flew, and before long the succulent smell of chicken soup was drifting through the Castle. I met the Poet once again as he made his way back up to Illyrica's room, cradling a bowl of soup in his hands, trying without entire success to keep from spilling hot drops of it and burning his hands.

Perhaps it was this act of faith of the Poet's that did it. I don't know. But it was only a short time later that Illyrica did fully awake, and before long Nora called for me.

Illyrica was sitting up in bed, smiling. Two little girls had climbed up into the bed next to her, and another stood leaning into the blankets with Illyrica's hand on her head. Nora sat on her other side, clasping her hand, while the Poet stood in the corner, an empty bowl on the table beside him, unable to keep himself from smiling.

Illyrica was very pale. The ugly gash on her neck from the gypsy's blow was bandaged. The gash would scar despite Nora's best efforts to prevent it, leaving Illyrica twice-marked as one who had escaped.

She looked up as I entered the room. Her eyes were a deeper, more serene blue than I had ever seen. She reached out for me, and I crossed the room to take her hand. She smiled radiantly up at me—saying "thank you." I bowed my head—in part to show my deep respect, and in lesser part to hide the tears in my eyes.

Illyrica released me. She leaned back and frowned. She looked up at Nora and made a sign with her hand which I knew meant "Pixie."

Nora nodded, stood, and crossed the room to the door. I think she meant to call for the Pixie, but it wasn't necessary— she was already there. She entered the room with a tearful smile and went to Illyrica's side with a self-consciousness that was very unlike her. Illyrica opened her arms, and the Pixie laid her head down on her shoulder. There was a lump growing in my throat. I found myself leaving the room.

It was not only the tears welling up in my eyes that drove me outside, nor the feeling that I was intruding. It was the fact that the Pixie's distress indicted me. I knew what she felt—what she heard. She could not erase the memories of her own recent opposition to the Giant, of the hurt she had caused to those who loved her. Moreover, she knew that the Widow's soldiers, accompanied by the Gypsy and his awful band, had literally followed her to the Castle door.

I burst out of the front door of the Castle into the cold air of the day. I had taken a bow and arrow from my room, and I made for the woods now, my thoughts whirling. Somehow, in trying to free Illyrica, I had managed to forget that it was I who had put her in danger in the first place. I had no right to forget. The guilt that was plaguing the Pixie should have been plaguing me. My own lack of penance made me angry. I charged into the forest in search of prey, found none, and realized I was near the hollow tree which the Widow had used to summon me.

At first I meant to ignore it, but curiosity got the better of me. I approached the tree—and found a summons waiting.

As usual, it was a handwritten note on parchment, requesting that I attend upon the Widow at my nearest convenience. It had been delivered the same day, probably late in the morning.

I meant to scorn it. But even as I tore the parchment and let the wind take the pieces, I made a very different decision. I would go again to Brawnlyn House, there to cut off every tie I had made with the Widow and her daughter.

Chapter 22

CHANGES (PART 2)

I MADE MY WAY UP THE LONG DRIVE to Brawnlyn House. The twisted, barren branches of the gardens seemed to reach out for me, the dead vines and intricately arranged stones covering the ground like some dormant evil. I turned my eyes from them and approached the doors, resolute. Every step I took was reproach to me. Alas that my feet should be so familiar with such a place! When last I had come this way, it had been in the full flush of pride. In one night I had betrayed the inhabitants of the Castle and exposed the Pixie to vanity, disappointment, and now, the destructive power of guilt. I wanted to tell her that the guilt was mine, but she had not let me speak with her since the night of the ball.

Lady Brawnlyn greeted me as ever she had. I bowed shortly, disdaining to step forward and kiss her hand. If she noticed my coldness, she did not show it. Genevieve was absent, for which I was glad.

There was a light in the Widow's eyes that I did not like, and a peculiar tone to her voice that filled me with aversion. "I am glad to see you," she said. "I feared it might be some time before you came our way again. I have heard rumours that you have been distinguishing yourself once again, my Lord Hawk. I had thought that perhaps your travels were taking you away from us."

Her eyes searched my face as she spoke, but I believe that I kept it impassive. A dark, dreadful calm was coming over me: the calm of certainty and disgust. I knew her words now for flattery, and I knew that they cloaked something deeper.

"Tell me," she said, "where is the Pixie? Surely this would be a fine time for her to accompany you."

My voice was tight, almost strangled. "She will not be coming this way again," I said.

The Widow raised her brow at me, but said nothing more on the subject. She leaned forward, dropping a cube of sugar into her tea. In doing so, she cast a deep shadow over the silver tray before her. I realized anew how dark the sitting room was, shrouded in drapes and carpeting, well hidden from the sun.

"It is just as well that you have come alone today," she said. "Hawk, hitherto you have served me well. Now I have a matter of great importance to give into your hands—of paramount importance, not only to the safety of this land, but to your own future happiness." She folded her hands and lowered her voice. "Tell me," she said, "what would you risk to recover a treasure—a fantastically great treasure—out of the hands of thieves? You must know that much of it would become yours."

It chilled me to know that, had she brought up such a thing only a short time ago, I would have been trapped by her spider's promise. More, I felt a pang of fear deep within me. Days ago I had watched a great treasure change hands. Could the Widow be speaking of any other?

"There is a thief," she said. "Someone hidden away in my lands who has gathered riches through extortion, blackmail, and robbery. Much has been taken even from the treasury of my own family: gold, Hawk, more than you can imagine. Its location has been kept a deep secret, but days ago a small part of the treasure came to the light. My guards found it in the possession of carnival men, careless drunkards who flaunted it stupidly, openly. Enough gold to buy up this house and all the land it sits on."

"Well, then," I said. "You have caught your thieves."

"No, Hawk, no," she said, the light in her eyes growing more strange and frightening. "They were vile, ignorant people, who obtained a piece of the treasure by their own vicious means—but no, they do not have it all. What they have is only a fraction. The treasure is much greater. It is great enough to make you the equal of any king."

She spoke to my old love of adventure; to my old greed for reknown. She spoke, moreover, to my fears and suspicions. I did not know how the Giant had come by the gold I had seen change hands. It might well have been by mercenary means. Yet I knew that, until I knew more, I could only trust him.

My pride had been broken, and with it, the Widow's power over me. I drew myself back, and her searching eyes meant the flint in mine with displeasure and some confusion. She had not thought me so far out of her reach.

"My lady," I said, "I did not come today to accept your commission—or any one of your words. How deeply you have been involved in the events of the past few days I cannot know, but I do know that I trust you no longer. You have no more control over me."

The Widow stood slowly. I felt small in her presence. "Take care, Hawk," she said. "Think of how much I have offered you. Think what alliance with me has brought you—will bring you!"

I did think of it. I thought of the Poet, still sitting at the foot of Illyrica's bed, and of the fear I had lately seen in Nora's eyes—for though she had not told me, I knew that she feared the Giant had given far more than he could afford in Illyrica's ransom. I thought of the Pixie, of the radiance she had lost as she sat caressing an old flour bag, of the freedom that had been torn from her when evil followed her home. I thought of myself and the traitorous wretch I had become.

"Widow Brawnlyn," I said, "you have brought me nothing but regret. From this day on I wish nothing more to do with you." I was nearly at the door. She raised her voice to me one last time.

"Consider, Hawk!" she said. "Consider well what you throw away!"

I opened the door and looked back at her. "You have *nothing* which could possibly tempt me," I said. "For you have nothing to offer that is of any true worth."

I turned and stormed out of the drawing room. I stopped short in the foyer. Genevieve stood on the stairway, looking down at me. We did not speak to one another. I turned and left Brawn-lyn House, as I thought, forever. I knew that Genevieve had heard my parting words. I could not be sure whether I was glad of it.

I said nothing to the people at the Castle about my visit to Widow Brawnlyn and her daughter. The further events of the day nearly drove it even from my mind. For it was on the same day, early in the evening when the sun was just beginning to die, that the Pixie packed up her few meager belongings and went away.

Chapter 23

I GO INTO EXILE

WINTER FOLDED ITS GREY WINGS and slept, and spring came to the Castle at last. The woods bloomed, the grass grew lush on the lawns, and the Castle turned nearly into the paradise it had been when I first came to it. But it was not truly the same. The Pixie's absence was constantly felt. Even the merriest of the little girls seemed subdued without her. Nora and I wanted to go out and look for her, but the Giant forbade us. I did not like his answer, but I had learned to trust him. In any case, I believed that he knew where she was and that she was safe.

The children were growing. Nora and Illyrica spent many an afternoon in the Castle or out on the lawns mending, taking out hems, altering sleeves, and darning stockings. Illyrica taught the Poet to use a needle, and he sat with them: sometimes helping them sew with his long fingers, sometimes playing the lute or reading to them as they worked. Only rarely was he away from Illyrica. The Giant, who had once limited the Poet's time at the Castle and restricted him to certain seasons, now allowed him to be with us constantly. I had no objection. He had earned it; he had proved his love.

Nora's eyes were weary in a way that I had not seen before. Perhaps it was that she missed the Pixie; perhaps she worried for the Giant and his secrets; perhaps it was simply that the care of the Castle was growing. I tried to ask her about it, but she waved me away.

It was just as well. The Castle's unorthodox family had faced many changes, but now at least they were at peace. The Giant still roamed the woods, protecting those he loved and keeping them supplied with food. I began to feel that they did not need me—that, moreover, I did not deserve to be among them. And so it was, as yellow flowers grew and white lilies-of-the-valley burst out all around the Castle and filled the air with their fragrance, that I sent myself into exile.

I told the Giant that I would be going. He nodded with hardly a word. I said a vague goodbye to the children, not caring if they saw the tears in my eyes as they threw their arms around my neck. I removed the arms of a four-year-old and tweaked her soft chin; stood up, and saw Nora step out of the kitchen.

She wiped her hands on her apron and looked at me quizzically.

I doffed my cap and said, "I'm leaving."

Nora frowned and looked away. "Why?" she asked.

"I—"

I licked my lips. I could not give her an explanation. I was not entirely sure why I was going away. "It is time I went," I said.

Nora nodded. She held out her hand. I took it and kissed it. "Safe journey, Sparrowhawk," she said.

I left her with a troubled heart. The sun was shining on a dew-jeweled world. Beneath the cherry trees the Poet was leading Illyrica by the hand and gesturing up to the blue sky. I took a step toward them to say goodbye, and found that I didn't have the heart. The little hawk tapestry Illyrica had given me for

Christmas was folded and tucked against my breast. I squared my shoulders and walked away. If they saw me go, I do not know. I didn't look back.

As I had come, in what seemed another lifetime, so I left. There was nothing in my dress to indicate that I was anything other than a common wanderer. I caught a ride on various farmers' carts. When I could not ride, I walked; when I could not walk, I slept; and when I could not sleep, I laid awake and tried to puzzle out what it had all meant—what the recent past had done to me, and what it would mean to my future. I could not tell.

After a journey of two weeks, I crested a ridge, sea wind in my hair. My old home lay before me, cold and impassive. Once an ancient fortress, its stone walls were surrounded by crumbling defenses. There was little activity on the brown, outlying moors. There rarely ever was. My family owned good farmland, but it was some distance away. The land around our home was desolate, and the sea that roared in the distance sang a stormy dirge over the landscape.

I presented myself to my uncle, the lord of the manor. He received me cordially, even with some familial gladness. When he called me by my real name, the syllables sounded strange in my ears.

"You are welcome home," he told me. "But I think it only fair to tell you that things have changed."

I had laid my cap on the table in front of me. I worked the cloth with my fingers. "Changed?" I asked.

"You have been gone some time," he said. "My boy, your aunt has at last given me a child. I have a son."

I felt the news more than I heard it, deep in the pit of my stomach. It meant that the land where I now stood would never be mine. I did not know why it should surprise me so. It had always been a possibility, after all—though one which most had long since given up on.

"Congratulations," I told him.

"You are of course welcome here," he said. "We have no intention of turning you or Sarah out."

"Thank you," I said. "It is good of you."

Sarah. My sister. I felt eyes on me even as the discussion came to an end. I turned to find her watching me with grave brown eyes. She was taller than when I had last seen her, her hair longer and just as straight as ever. She wore a brown dress that fell to her ankles. The hem of it was a little stained and torn from walking the moors.

"Hello, Sarah," I said. I walked over to her and kissed her cheek. She did not respond. Instead, she looked at me as though she was trying to remember who I was.

"I thought you were dead," she said at last.

"No," I told her. "No, I am very much alive. How—how old are you now?"

"Thirteen," she told me.

"Ah." I nodded. She was a stranger to me. She always had been. We had grown up together, but I had never before seen anything in her to pay much attention to. I had left her to my aunt and the occasional nurse.

My uncle was good to me. When he saw that I would go crazy with idleness, he gave me work to do. I spent many of my days in the city, many miles off, representing the estate to the bankers and businessmen there. It was a wearisome job. I found myself longing for the woods, for the lawns, for the shining white walls of the Castle. When I returned home, my ears strained to hear the sound of laughter or the Pixie plucking a lute to call the children into the soft room. Dressed in starched, straight clothes, I missed the humble ways of the little paradise I had left. As I had done in the past, I took to riding bareback by the sea, letting the surf and the endless grey at once soothe and exacerbate my loneliness.

Sarah did little to alleviate my sense of isolation. She was a peculiar child, odd as they are who are young and too much alone. There were no other children anywhere near; she had no friends. I wondered if she ever had. The old manor had many secret passageways and hidden tunnels of a nature not unusual in such an old house, and Sarah knew them all. She had a way of turning up underfoot, to stand and watch without a word, and then disappearing again.

One night I returned from riding, soaked with sea spray, to find Sarah sitting on the floor at the foot of my bed. She was examining a piece of cloth by lamplight.

I strode across the room and opened the heavy drapes, letting the fading evening light fill the room. Without a word I pushed the windows wide open, scattering sea birds and allowing the distant sound of waves to reach us. Then I turned to look at Sarah. I could see now what she was holding. It was Illyrica's picture.

Sarah pointed to the white house in its bed of verdant green. "Where is this?" she asked. Her words were clipped short, as they always were.

"That is the Castle," I said. I lowered myself down to the floor beside her, and pointed to the woods. "And these are the woods where the Angel lives."

She looked up at me without smiling. "Why does he live there?" she asked.

"He protects the girls who live in the Castle," I said. "There are many of them, and every one is a princess."

Sarah ran her thumb along the grey and white and brown threads that made up the hawk. "And what does the hawk do?" she asked.

"He watches over the Castle," I told her. "And they teach him how to fly."

We fell silent as the sun set over the sea, deepening the shadows around the bed. We could hear birds crying over the surf. Somewhere in the moors cattle were lowing.

"That's me," I said suddenly. "They called me Hawk."

Her brown gaze was unwavering. "Then why are you here?" she asked.

I looked at her, brown and serious in the deepening eve. And I knew why I had come back. I smiled, an awkward smile, and touched her cheek. "I came back for you," I said.

She looked back down at the picture and picked up the lamp again to shed light over the threads. "Will we go back there?" she asked.

"Yes," I told her.

Chapter 24

NORA

WITH SARAH IN MY CARE, the journey back took twice as long. Alone, I had been willing to forego meals and walk long miles, but I was determined that Sarah should not go hungry. At many places along the road I stopped and worked in the fields for hire, paying our way across the provinces. When I had done particularly well, we would sometimes even sleep in an inn. Although Sarah was given to wandering the moors alone at home, she did not like to be out at night. The world was too big for her then. She was accustomed to burrowing in her tunnels and cubby holes at night, and the open blackness frightened her. Whenever we slept out of doors, I would find a low-hanging branch—or else gather sticks and build a framework—and drape my cloak over it so that she had something between her and the night.

The result of our slow progress was that summer was half-spent by the time we reached the edge of the darkwood. It was now nearly the season in which I had lived in the woods under the Giant's tutelage. The world under the canopy of leaves began to tantalize my senses the moment I stepped beneath the trees. Everything was thrillingly familiar and inexplicably strange; like entering a world one has known only in dreams—good dreams. Sarah's eyes were wide as we followed the nearly invisible paths into the forest. She was searching it out, taking in every sound and movement and scent. This was a wilderness very different from the moors, and well I knew it.

The sun was just beginning to set as the trees thinned and I caught sight of the glimmer of white walls. "Look there," I told Sarah. "There is the Castle."

"I can't see it," she told me.

"Well then," I said, and swooped her suddenly off her feet. I lifted her to my shoulder as she kicked and clutched at my head in shock and nervous fear. And then, in a beautiful moment that I would ever after remember, she laughed. It was a small laugh, born as much from relief that I was holding her securely as from surprise, but it was a laugh.

"Can you see it now?" I asked her.

There was silence. I turned my face up to see her. She was staring off through the trees, brown eyes deep, a small smile playing on her face. "Yes," she said. "I can see it."

With Sarah still on my shoulder, I started to walk toward the Castle. She tightened her hold with hands and knees, but made no protest. I stopped short when we stepped out of the trees. The Castle sat on its hill, glimmering all the colours of pearl in the light of the setting sun. Clouds heaped in the sky made the sunlight fall in beautiful golden waves over the lawns, and there a lone figure walked. Her hands were slightly outstretched, palms turned up, as though they would take in all the glory of the fading day.

It was Nora. She had let her hair down, as I had only seen it once before, and it fell in long tresses to her waist. Her skirts flowed out behind her. Sarah's hands came around my forehead as she leaned forward. A warm breeze began to blow, as though it was running to Nora's open hands. It pushed her hair away from her face and made the long strands dance.

Something alerted Nora to our presence. She turned, and even from such a distance I thought I could see the quickening blue of her eyes. For a moment she seemed confused—andand then she broke into a radiant smile and began to hurry across the grass toward us.

"Hawk?" she called when she was near, but her eyes were on Sarah.

I didn't know what to say. There had never been much use in flowery words with Nora. "I've brought my sister," I told her. "Sarah."

Nora reached up and took Sarah's hands with a smile. I knelt down, and Nora helped Sarah off my shoulder. "Welcome," she told her, and impulsively put her arms around her and pressed Sarah's motherless head to her breast.

I knew in that moment that my old dream of falling wildly and instantly in love with some exotic beauty would never be realized, for I loved Nora; and it had happened slowly and prosaically. The boy I had been almost regretted it—an adventure I had yearned for was forever beyond my grasp. But the man I was becoming knew that the deepest and truest things in the world are not often won in whirlwind adventures. Nora started toward the house with her arm around Sarah's shoulders, and as I watched them go, I felt my heart straining—surely it was so full that it could never be small or petty again.

It seemed to me that there were eyes on me. I turned and saw a shadowy figure just beyond the treeline.

I smiled, for I knew there was a smile on the Angel's face.

PART 2

Chapter 25

RETROSPECT

THE YEAR THAT FOLLOWED my return to the Castle was marked by change. Illyrica and the Poet were married on the rolling front lawn of the Castle, with Nora and the Giant as their attendants. They had a long train of little girls in befrilled dresses, flowers twined in their hair, to dance and skip about them. The woods had reached the crowning height of autumn glory. Illyrica, angelic in a golden gown, went to meet her husband down a grassy aisle jeweled with leaves of brilliant red, yellow, and orange. The older girls, Isabelle and Sarah among them, watched the proceedings with a shy delight that was nevertheless fierce. Perhaps, for the first time, they thought of their own futures. We missed the Pixie.

As Illyrica reached the head of the aisle, she turned to hand her bouquet to Nora, and I saw the look that passed between them: love, joy, and the sadness of those who together say goodbye to their old lives. Illyrica turned and joined hands with the Poet, and an era ended. She was beautiful; white-gold hair curling down her back, blue eyes radiant. The thin white scars that twice marred her throat marked her as a treasure of great value—precious as only one can be who has nearly been lost.

The Poet, for all his genius, proved to be of some practical use after all. He set himself to farming a little plot of land on the edge of the darkwood, near the town, and to raising a small flock of chickens. He and Illyrica settled into a cottage covered with vines, half a mile from the farmland and practically on top of the chickens.

Winter came upon us, burying us seemingly away from the world. At first it was as it had been the year before. I stayed at the Castle, helping break ice and draw water, chop firewood, and fix anything the harshness of the season or the carelessness of girl-children saw fit to break. My sister was often by my side, with Isabelle generally at hers, my shadow trailed by a shadow. I was perfectly happy, for there in the Castle I could keep my eye on those things which mattered most to me: on the way Sarah was slowly becoming a real, warm human being, on the children as they laughed and played and grew, and on the way Nora lived out every moment of every day.

But a month had not passed before this changed. The Giant summoned me out to the woods with him. Once more I was in training: learning, this time, how to stay hidden in a world of white, how to survive in a world of cold, and how to defend the Castle in winter. I learned quickly. How my pride had hindered me before, and I had not known it! Before winter was half-over the Giant began to leave me alone to guard the woods while he rested by the fire in the Castle. We fell into a routine, trading off every few days. Loath though I was to be away from Nora, I was glad to take the Giant's place. I saw for the first time the grey in his hair and the lines in his face. I knew that his time sitting by the fire was doing him a world of good. Now and then, when the Giant felt that something was amiss, we both attended to the woods, roaming guardians over twice the land that one could cover.

The Giant was not without cause for concern, for while the winter was quiet and uneventful for us, the outside world was not so fortunate. News came in on the snowy wind, often given to us by the Poet through his thick wool muffler. Late in the fall, a villager had been struck down by plague. Since then it had spread. Few families were unaffected. At the same time, the roving bands of thieves whom the Widow had declared so characteristic of her province were growing bolder. For the townspeople, that winter was a long struggle against death.

When the struggle broke, the Pixie came back to us.

It was a grey, rainy day in March. Nora was sitting at an upstairs window looking out on the dismal grey-green world, when she started up with a cry and ran for the door. I looked and saw what she had seen: a lone figure, wrapped in a tattered scarf with its ends blowing in the wind, unmistakable red-gold hair blowing with it. And something in her arms, wrapped tightly in a scarf, and clutched very closely to her.

Nora and I met her together as she struggled up the hill. Her boots and stocking were covered in mud, the hem of her skirt past repair. She smiled when she saw us, but her eyes filled with tears. Nora embraced her the moment she reached her, and then leaned over and exclaimed at the bundle in the Pixie's arms. It was a baby.

The Pixie looked up and saw me. She smiled at the look on my face. "And you, Hawk!" she said. "Have you never seen a baby before? Come, old friend. Are you well?"

"I am," I stammered. "And you…"

"Are home," Nora cut in. "And you must come and dry out before another word is said."

The Pixie nodded. Her smile was weary. Nora took the baby from her, and the Pixie stumbled, as though, with her precious burden removed, she was free to collapse. I moved forward quickly and caught her arm. She leaned on me. I saw in an instant how thin and weak she was.

She told us the story that night in front of the fire, after the children had been sent to bed. She had gone to live with a crofter and his wife, Kate, true friends she had long ago met in the marketplace in the town. They had lived there happily enough, though she was constantly weighed down with guilt and shame when she thought of the Castle. Often she missed it, but she would not come home—not until she had reached some peace within herself.

Then the plague had come, and the crofter was struck down. Kate was the next to take ill. The Pixie had spent the winter vainly trying to nurse her friend back to health while caring for Kate's little one. At last Kate died, and the Pixie found that she herself was ill. Racked by pain and fever, half-starved and alone, the Pixie lived only to keep the baby alive. She had succeeded, and when she was certain that she posed no risk to any healthy person, she had come home.

Nora cried all through the story, and I sat with my fingers clenched tightly. I knew that Nora and I agreed—we should have been there. The Pixie, our Pixie, should not have been alone. Yet she had been… and somehow, it was for the best.

"When I awoke from my illness," the Pixie told us, "the old guilt was gone. Looking death in the face reminded me that life was waiting. Ironic, isn't it?"

She laughed, a low laugh that contained echoes of her girlhood. She looked down and traced the baby's cheek in the firelight. A lump grew in my throat. I had witnessed a miracle, something that can only be compared to the change of a chrysalis. The Pixie, foolhardy girl who had so captured my imagination, had become a woman.

Chapter 26

A DEEP CONTENT

RUNNING ITS COURSE NEAR the castle was a creek, its waters glistening in a perpetual twilight beneath the long drooping boughs of the weeping willows. Various members of the gaggle had taken to calling it "the river." Nora's bedtime stories had often featured rivers of late, some of them home to lovely water sprites; others wild and white, barring the way to far-off lands; one an ancient bard calling its lovely song over the stones in its path. The little ones were quite captured by these rivers, and naturally wanted one of their own.

Our river was not an exciting place in itself, but at times its lovely green shadows deepened, and it suddenly became something uncanny: too still and ancient to belong to this world. Or so the Pixie told me. She often sat by the water, cradling the tiny one in her arms, and watching an old dream take shape beneath the willows: a boat. None of the children could remember whose idea the boat had first been. It seemed to have come upon them all at once, and stayed with remarkable tenacity.

The boat was now in its third year. The first year, they had set out to build it with a vengeance. When several attempts had failed, they lost interest. The following spring, when the ice melted off the creek and the willows came out of their barren sleep, the passion returned. But that had been an unfortunate year, with enough rain in April to thoroughly drench the gaggle and their dreams, and send them off, sodden and muddy, to other pursuits. I had come that year, and with me renewed hope, but the Giant had whisked me into training in the woods.

In the spring that the Pixie returned to us, the boat-dream once more came to life. This time, it was Sarah who orchestrated its revival. She and Isabelle were wandering by the creek one day when they found the remains of an old attempt, and Isabelle poured out the tragic story. Sarah, who of all the girls drank in Nora's stories with all of her soul and strength, at once decided that the boat would sail—that it must.

Sarah had a strong practical streak that aided, rather than thwarting, her determination. She came to me, Isabelle and three younger girls behind her, and announced their intent. "But they've tried to build it before and been a sad failure," she told me. "I told them you would help us."

She said so in a tone of absolute confidence, but when I looked at her I saw a tiny note of uncertainty in her brown eyes. "You can build and carry things better than we can," she said.

I smiled and stood, stretching. "Of course I'll help," I said.

We met Nora on the way out. She was on her hands and knees in the garden by the side of the Castle. She looked up and wiped sweat away from her eyes, streaking her brow with dirt, and smiled as the girls called to her in great excitement. "Nora, Nora, we're going to build a boat and sail down the river!" She looked up at me, and I smiled and said, "That we are."

She looked back down and plunged a bulb into the dirt. "Be back in time for dinner," she said, still smiling to herself in some enjoyment that I felt I was beginning to understand. There was a joy in involving myself in the concerns and desires of the little girls that I had never imagined—a rightness in loving them, and even in serving them. Nora had lived that way for years, and I knew now why she so loved it. I felt also a deep joy in knowing her, in being there to work alongside her though she did not care for me as I did for her. The life I had entered had become to me a deep content.

By the bank of the creek, I helped the girls gather old logs and lash them together. We launched the boat that same afternoon, and it promptly sank. The look on Sarah's face told me that the venture was far from over. Truth be told, I felt it keenly myself when the logs disappeared beneath the water. The girls splashed into the creek with yelps and laughter to fetch it, but it was waterlogged and too heavy for them. They straggled back to shore with their dresses soaked, looking up at me.

"We'll build another," I said.

Sarah stepped forward, ringing water from her petticoats. "Hawk," she said, "you watched the shipwrights where we used to live. Can't we build a boat like they did?"

As a boy I had gone down to the villages by the sea and watched more than one old salt transform pieces of lumber into a seaworthy vessel. I could, I thought, build a rowboat—perhaps even something with a small sail on it. How difficult could it be?

Into the work I plunged, always with Sarah helping wherever she could, and the other girls variously standing half-underfoot and taking orders from my little sister and me. Isabelle proved to have a good eye for what should be done next. She sometimes reminded me of what I had seen in the villages by suggesting this thing or that. What I had expected to be the work of an hour became the labour of weeks. We found a tree and chopped it down, transformed the wood into useable lumber, and learned by trial and error what tools we needed. Whenever we had a free moment, various of us would gather beneath the willows and work. Even Nora would sometimes leave her responsibilities and watch us, always with the little ones holding her hands or leaning over her shoulders.

On the third day of every other week, Nora left the Castle altogether. She who had once lived every minute there now ventured out often—had been doing so for months. She went out to visit the most unlikely person imaginable: Genevieve Brawnlyn. The first time she announced her intention to go, I had tried my best to dissuade her. But Nora was determined, and the Angel approved. I had not returned to Brawnlyn House since the day I cut ties with the widow and her daughter. In my memory Genevieve seemed to be something inhuman—a malevolent creature of storm and ice. But the Pixie, before going away from us, had told Nora a little of Genevieve, and Nora's heart had pitied her. Sometimes I thought Nora saw her as one of her rescued girls, only she hadn't quite made it into the Castle's fold, and so rescue had to go out to her.

Knowing what I did of Genevieve, I expected that Nora would be repulsed. Surely the proudly beautiful young woman would not be pitied. But Nora went with the grace of a visiting noblewoman. She was, after all, mistress of a Castle. And Genevieve, as far as I could tell, received her as such. What they did or talked about I did not know; I knew that Nora often came back troubled, and a little grieved. And though she and I had become friends—with both the Pixie and Illyrica away from the Castle, Nora had grown to need me a little—we never spoke of her visits.

Chapter 27

THE ATTACK

IT WAS A COOL EVENING late in May. I stood bent over my makeshift workbench by the creek, my short sleeves rolled up past my shoulders, sanding the uncooperative forebear of a rowboat plank. Wild apple trees were flowering in the woods nearby. A sudden breeze caught the blossoms up and carried them through the willow branches. White petals floated down around me, and I heard my name on the breeze. What young voice had called, I could not tell. I put my work down and waited.

They came in a moment, stumbling over roots in their path: four of the girls, their faces flushed and happy. They had already swept Sarah up in their plans. She had been downstream, sewing together the various scraps of cloth Nora had given us for a sail.

"Pixie says she will take us to see Illyrica if you will come, Hawk," said the leader of the little ones. I set the uncooperative plank aside.

"That sounds like a fine plan," I answered. "Are we all here? Where's Isabelle?"

A voice came from the direction of the apple trees, and Isabelle's dark head appeared on the other side of the creek. "Here," she said. "I'll go, too." She turned and ran toward a narrower part of the creek, where she clambered across the stepping stones and joined the rest of the party.

The smallest girls grabbed onto my hands, and together we made our way to the Castle lawn, where the Pixie stood waiting for us. She greeted us with a radiant smile. Little Katie, dressed in white with a bright blue kerchief tied around her blonde head, was playing in the grass at the Pixies feet. Isabelle ran forward, and at a nod from the baby's guardian, scooped the little one up and balanced her on her hip.

Through the woods we went, the girls laughing and chattering, the Pixie and I hushed by the beauty of the darkwood in late spring. Several times the Pixie looked back to see if Isabelle showed any sign of wanting to give the baby up, but no matter how Katie sagged on her hip, Isabelle seemed always ready to jostle her back up again and keep going.

The day could not have been more pleasant, and so the walk seemed short. As we reached the cottage some of the girls broke out ahead out of the group, running and laughing, to see who would be first to knock on the old wooden door. The vines that covered the cottage were in bloom. The chickens were underfoot as ever. The girls needn't have bothered to knock, for Illyrica appeared from behind the cottage, wiping her hands in her apron and smiling in welcome. She held out her hands to the girls, silently greeting each of them in turn, and then to the Pixie. I nodded my greeting and inquired after her husband.

Illyrica turned her head and with her eyes indicated the path I should follow. As it was the way to the farm fields, I assumed I would find the Poet at work, carving his book of love into the earth—not with a pen but with a plough.

I found him coming back, grimy with dirt and sweat, his old billowy sleeves torn and patched and torn again. He greeted me with an enormous smile and clapped me on the shoulder. "Glorious day, isn't it?" he said.

"It is," I answered, and together we turned and walked back toward the cottage.

"Have I told you about my newest composition?" he said. I shook my head, amused, and he carried on. "I have been all month wrestling with the plough, and it has been all month speaking to me. I am writing a long poem, more of a collection of poems, really. I call it *Songs of the Field*." His face fell a little. "The title lacks poetry. I find it hard to capture all this in words."

"The title may lack poetry," I said. "I am sure the book itself does not."

He brightened immediately. "Oh, no, no," he said. "Of course it does not. I read them to my wife every night before the fire, and I think… I think she likes them."

"I'm sure she loves them," I answered.

All this time there had been in the distance an unusual clamour of chickens, but only now did it strike me that there was something odd about it. In the next moment, a scream tore through the spring stillness. In an instant we were running down the path. We could not move quickly enough. We burst out of the foliage into the clearing where the cottage was. The Poet was to it and through the door in seconds. Another scream halted me in my tracks. I recognized the voice as Sarah's. I looked to see her standing twenty feet from the cottage door, eyes wildly searching for something. They lighted on me.

"Hawk!" she called. "Come quick!"

I saw a flash of movement in the woods beyond her and ran forward. I snatched Sarah up and bore her back to the cottage, all but shoving her through the door. The others were all there.

The Pixie and Isabelle grabbed Sarah the instant she passed the threshold. "What were you *doing?*" the Pixie scolded, and Sarah looked back at her with smouldering eyes.

"Calling Hawk back," she said. "It worked. He's here!"

"What's going on?" I demanded. In answer Illyrica took my arm and pointed out the unshuttered window.

Once again I saw movement in the woods, and then in another spot. I squinted, trying to focus beyond the trees. I could see them now—there were men in the woods, several of them, circling the cottage like wolves on the hunt. They wore no livery. From what I could see they were unkempt, but well-armed.

Thieves.

The Poet appeared at my elbow, having taken down a large sword that usually hung over the fireplace. In a low whisper, I told him what was happening and pointed out the men I could see. There were at least four of them. I had come to the cottage unarmed. I turned and scanned the room, passing over the girls who were huddled together with the Pixie and Illyrica hovering above them, and caught sight of the iron poker for the fireplace. I stood, took up the poker, and turned back toward the door. The Poet started toward it as though he would go out and face them. I stopped him with a word.

"No," I said. "Let them come out where we can see them first."

The Poet was sweating. "Do you think they'll take the chance? They know we're in here."

"And they know there's only two of us," I said. "They won't be patient."

I was right. Twenty minutes had not passed before their leader emerged from the woods, riding a black pony. He wore a mask over his face. His long dark hair and tall form gave an impression of youth and strength. Behind him, six others moved out from the green cover of the trees, all of them on foot; unmasked, uncouth, unhappy men. I did not know any of them from my days working for the Widow, and it occurred to me suddenly that they were new to the area—or at least new to thievery. They lacked the careless indolence of those who habitually live off of the work of others. There was too much anger in their faces, too much desperation. My heart sank. We might be in for a harder battle than I had at first anticipated.

"Seven against two," the Poet whispered near my ear.

"Three," I told him. "The Angel will not be long."

My answer, I hoped, was more comfort to him than it was to me. Admire the Poet though I did, I had no great faith in his ability to fight. For now, I might as well have been on my own.

The man on horseback reached up and drew his sword from a sheath strapped to his back. He rode forward a few feet and shouted, "Surrender!"

I heard a whimper behind me and turned to see the girls huddled together, all of them pale and frightened—even the Pixie. "The loft," I said.

The Pixie heard me. "What?" she asked, loosening her hold on the girls just a little.

I had remembered that above our heads was a bit of a loft—little more than a crawl space. But the girls might be safe there if the thieves were to force their way in. I motioned to the ceiling with my head. "Up to the loft, all of you!" I said.

Illyrica nodded and led the way. The Poet watched them go, and I trained my eyes back on the thieves. I was crouched near the window; I knew they could hear me as I shouted back.

"Keep away," I said. "There's nothing for you here."

The eyes behind the mask narrowed. "I don't believe you," the man called back. Without warning he spurred his horse, sword in hand, and charged at the door.

I was out the door at the same moment that I heard a sound like glass breaking above me. An arrow streaked through the air, over my head, and hit the rider's shoulder. Whether it wounded him or not I cannot say, but it caught him off guard, and knocked him off balance. He was no great horseman, as I could now see. His attention thus diverted, I ran straight for him and swung the poker into his side. The next moment he was rolling in the dirt. The pony had bolted in another direction.

He scrambled to close his fingers around the hilt of his sword. I was not fast enough to stop him. He was on his feet, and swinging the sword at me, before I could think what to do next. I blocked his every blow with the poker: hard blows. He was strong and fast, but my old training was still good, and he was not better with a sword than the Giant had been with a staff in the woods. From the corner of my eye I could see the Poet, wildly swinging his sword, surrounded. Desperately, I dropped low and swung the poker at my opponent's knees. He landed heavily on his back. I had no time to defeat him finally: I was already running to the Poet's aid. I bashed the sword from another thief's hand, picked it up, and slashed at another. The Poet and I stood back to back, barely able to hold our enemies at bay.

The man whose sword I had taken ran for the woods, perhaps in search of another weapon. But in a moment he returned: flailing unceremoniously through the air and landing on his nose in the dirt with a terrified screech. The Angel roared out of the forest, his eyes like flames in his anger. His staff caught another of our foes in the stomach and sent him flying.

The fight was over within minutes. The thieves scattered, running for their lives.

Except one. The man I had felled lay still in the dirt.

The door of the cottage burst open and the girls came running. I stood looking down at the masked thief who lay at my feet. The corner of an old foundation stone jutted out of the ground where he had fallen. The ground around his head was growing dark with blood.

The Pixie appeared at my side. Her face was flushed. She had wrapped her skirt around her hand like a bandage. She looked at me silently. The Poet came up beside her, Illyrica clinging to him.

I knelt down slowly and took the man's head and shoulders up in my arms.

"He is dead," I said.

I felt a hand on my shoulder: the Angel. He looked solemnly down at me.

Carefully, I took the edge of the mask and peeled it away. The face was young, handsome, still holding the vestiges of boyhood. It was not a face made for thievery and violence. The Pixie gasped.

"Do you know him?" the Angel asked.

She nodded. "He is the son of the town wainwright," she said. "Most of his family was lost to the plague."

"Does his father still live?" the Angel asked.

The Pixie nodded.

"Then we must return the boy's body to him," I said.

"Yes. But not before we have seen the girls safely back to the Castle," the Angel said. "The others may return… though I think it unlikely."

I nodded and laid the young man's body back down on the ground. I was shaking as I stood. I turned, noticing the Pixie's bandaged hand again. There were traces of blood on her arm above the skirt ends she'd wrapped around it.

"What happened?" I asked.

"It's nothing," she said. "I cut my hand a little... putting it through the window in the loft."

"The arrow," I said, remembering. "You won the battle for us."

"Not me," the Pixie said. "I only opened up the way."

"Then who...?" I asked.

The Pixie smiled and nodded at the child who stood apart from the little huddle of girls behind us. Sarah. She stood very straight and still, and swallowed as she looked at me. There were tears in her brown eyes.

"You did well, Sarah," I said. "You saved us all. You did well."

I reached out, and she came forward and took my hand. She tucked her head against my waist as I pulled her close.

"Come," I said, and raised my eyes to the others also. "Let's go home."

Chapter 28

————◆◆◆————

PORTENT

WHEN WE HAD SETTLED the girls at home, the Angel and I returned to the Poet's cottage. Its master and mistress we left behind to watch over the little ones while Nora washed and bandaged the Pixie's hand. At the Angel's direction, I hitched up the pony to a long two-wheeled cart, usually used for hauling wood. He laid a blanket of grey and green wool over it and slapped the pony gently. We made our way back in grim silence. The outer calm of the woods, of the pony's clopping hooves, of our very manner belied the strange turmoil inside me. I could still feel the fading rush of fear and determination that had come over me when I first heard Sarah's scream. Sadness mingled with the knowledge, almost the pride, that I had done what had to be done. Yet within these emotions was another, alienated from everything else in me, like a high, thin banner waving somewhere in the thin air of my heart. *A man was dead.* And though my weapon—poor, ridiculous poker!—had not killed him, I knew myself responsible for his death.

The yard was a haunted picture of itself as we approached, wagon wheels bumping over the earth. The cottage, with its shattered window; chickens scratching at the earth. A scene only slightly altered, eerie in its quiet normalcy. And the dead man, younger even than I remembered him, lying where he had fallen.

My heart wrenched as we drew near.

The Angel lifted the young man's body. Together we wrapped it in the blanket. The Angel raised his hand to strike the pony again, but I saw his hand shake, and grief flashed across his face. Without a word he unhitched the pony and took up the cart himself. We started toward the town.

The earth around the yard was scuffed with footprints. The Angel looked down at them and frowned. "They came back," he said.

"Why did they not take the body?" I asked.

The Angel closed his eyes. Again I saw grief written in the lines of his face. "I cannot speak for other men," he said. Of course. I wondered how much the Angel and other men could even understand each other. I remembered what Nora had told me of the Angel's past on the night we followed Illyrica's captors. He had lost something in his life, and out of his loss he had poured himself out to care for others. The young one we now carried home, along with his friends, had lost much—and out of their grief had turned to thievery. No, there could be little understanding between them.

One thing they did have in common: loss. I could see the grief of it now in the Angel's face as he mourned over one he had never known.

The sun was sinking low and a pallor falling over the world as we neared the town. We heard a clatter of wheels as we saw them: a coach, drawn by black horses, coming toward us. We slowed down as it came closer, unwilling to leave the road, but it neither slowed nor swerved. At last we stopped by the side of the road and waited. The coach bore down on us and pulled to a sudden, sharp stop next to us.

Men rode within and without. A young fellow sat hunched next to the driver, sullen and sallow. I thought I recognized him from the attack on the house. But another man commanded all of our attention as he descended from within the coach. The wainwright. His face was thin, haggard, drawn with hardship. But it was his eyes that were most striking. They seemed hollowed out and filled again with something wild. He fixed them on us and then looked slowly, deliberately, at our cargo.

"Give me my son," he said. His voice was choked.

"My friend," the Angel began.

The wainwright held up his hand. "Monster," he spat. "Give me my son."

The Angel looked at me. I stepped over and took the handles of the cart. I bent my head as the weight of it fell on me. I did not want to look into the father's face.

The Angel stooped down and lifted the body gently, handing it to the wainwright. The man turned without a word, staggering slightly under the weight. Several men jumped down from the wagon to help him. They pulled away without another word to us. We stood in the road and watched them make their unhappy way back. The Angel shook his head, but did not give voice to his thoughts. As I watched the convoy go, a faint glimmer of recognition came to me. I had seen the coach before—and the horses. They belonged to the Widow Brawnlyn.

The hostile exchange did not leave my mind that day, or for days afterward. For once I knew that my thoughts ranged the same ground as the Angel's. But it was not until two weeks had passed that I realized there would be trouble.

I had cut my forearm several days earlier while working on the boat, and the wound had become infected. It did not seem to me dangerous, but Nora was not happy with it. She knew of an herb she was convinced would set it to rights, but she had neglected to plant any. One day she wrapped herself in her shawl, took a basket, and walked to the town to visit a woman who dealt in herbs and medicines.

The woman received her hesitantly, her eyes darting about as if she feared being watched. She gave Nora what she wanted in a rush. Nora left, puzzled, and was passing down the main street when something stung her. She clasped her arm and whirled around, dropping her basket in time to sidestep a second rock as it flew past her shoulder. The townspeople had moved back from her, almost surrounding her. She could not pick out her assailant from the sea of hostile faces.

A bigger rock hit her in the shoulder blade and nearly knocked her off balance. A voice shrieked out from the crowd. "Murderess!"

"No," Nora said, as more rocks and dirt began to fly.

"Get out!" a man shouted. "Get out!"

She took his advice. Narrowly avoiding a stone aimed for her head, she picked up her basket and ran. A voice called after her, dogging her footsteps all the way back to the Castle: "Go home, girl! But don't think you're safe!"

It was those words that she related to us later that evening as she sat, a little bruised and more than a little shaken, in the soft room. The Pixie sat beside her, one hand clutching Nora's tightly, the other hand using a soft, damp cloth to wash away the dirt that smeared Nora's face and neck where a rock had grazed her. The Angel and I sat side by side, listening to her. The Angel's eyes were half-closed. His whole bearing spoke of sadness. I sat with my arms crossed, fists clenched at my sides. I was calm; so calm, but inwardly I was raging. How could they? How could anyone? Every time I closed my eyes I saw Nora, she who was, as the Pixie had long ago said, "All of our mother, and sister, and best friend in the world," stoned out of town and hideously accused. When I opened them again she was there in the firelight, still shaken, bruises and welts a reminder that it had really happened.

I stood suddenly. I could not stand to sit still. She looked up at me, her blue eyes pleading, and to the Angel as she spoke. "Something's going to happen," she said. "They're going to come after us, I can feel it."

"We will be ready for them," I said. *Murderess*, they had called her. At that moment I felt I could have happily murdered any one of them.

"That we will." The Angel reached out and his laid his big hand over Nora and the Pixie's interlocked fingers. He smiled sadly. I saw the fear and tension melt away from Nora's eyes. She was a child again, trusting the one who had always taken care of her. "Don't worry," he said. "We will be ready.

Chapter 29

WE WITHDRAW

WE HELD NO COUNCIL OF WAR, but we who count-ed ourselves protectors of the Castle knew that conflict could not be long avoided. We set about preparing in our own ways. Nora led the girls—all of them—into the half-wild or-chards around the lawns, where they spent the day perched in the tree tops, calling to each other and laughing as they pruned, trimmed, and readied the trees to do without us for a while. The Pixie oversaw the transplanting of tomato plants and flowering vines from the outlying gardens to vegetable beds beneath the eaves of the Castle. She gave orders with Katie tied up in a bundle on her back, tangling her little fists in the Pixie's long hair. Isabelle and Sarah carried the smaller plants all the way into the Castle, where they crowded every windowsill and raised more than one eyebrow. Nora had other gardens in the woods, where nuts and wild roots were already edible. She saw to it that everything was harvested that could be. The Giant disappeared early, patrolling the woods, but I knew he was near the little band of harvesters as they worked.

I spent a good deal of time patrolling, pitched in with the apple trees, and brought every weapon the Castle could claim into places where they could be easily reached. There were sev-eral swords. I sharpened them, bent over the whetstone in the yard behind the Castle, with sweat running into my eyes. Summer was coming. I could feel it in the air. Never before had the growing heat of the sun felt so ominous. Nora saw me at work as she passed through the yard on her way to the kitchen. Emotion swept across her face before she could stop it. I looked up from the blade to her, willing her to understand that I had never wanted any of this to happen—that I was as eager to preserve peace as she.

She looked away and touched the bruise on her neck absently. My stomach tightened at the sight. But she looked back at me, and nodded a little. She did understand. When she emerged from the kitchen again it was with bandages and herbs to tend the cut on my arm, which was still infected and growing more painful every day.

"It should have healed before this," Nora said, her voice strained as she changed the bandage.

"Nora," I said. She looked up at me. Her blue eyes were full of pain.

"It's going to be all right," I said.

She nodded and tried to smile. "I know."

The little girls did not understand what was happening, but they knew it was important. They pitched in as best they could, short legs running the distance between woods and Castle, little skirts and aprons full of wild roots and carefully cradled vegetable plants. In the late afternoon most of them threw themselves down on the green grass of the lawn, rested their faces in the crooks of their elbows, and giggled and whined and whispered by turns until they fell asleep. Still the Pixie passed by them with her carts and moving gardens, and voices called from the trees, and out in dark shadows of the woods the Giant watched.

The older ones had a better idea of the way things stood. In the golden light of early evening I caught sight of movement at the edge of the lawn. I smiled to myself as I made out Sarah and Isabelle straining to drag the unfinished boat up the hill to the safety of the Castle. I went out to help them, and we tucked it inside an old, mostly unused cellar behind the kitchen.

As we emerged, we saw three figures making their way toward us: the Angel with the Poet and Illyrica. He had convinced them to come to the Castle for their own safety. I met the Poet with a handclasp, trying to reassure him. His farm was behind him, and though he meant to tend it every day, it was at the mercy of—of whatever might happen.

Thus we withdrew from the world. By the end of the day most of the work was finished. As the sun sank down beneath the horizon, both the Giant and I slipped away from the Castle into the darkness of the forest. If danger came to us, it would come through the woods.

I turned back to see the lights shining from the windows of the Castle, golden across its pale walls. The moonrise was reflected in the white stones. I remembered with a sudden pang the first time I had seen it: a light in the middle of the darkwood, guarded by its terrible guardian, keeper of so many joys and so many secrets. I had imagined then so many things that it might come to mean to me, but never had I imagined the reality. I had thought the Castle might make me a hero, an adventurer, a great and splendid figure. Never had I imagined that it would teach me, so quietly and so sweetly, to love.

But I loved it now, and every one who rested within its walls. I loved the little ones, and the Pixie who had first drawn me to this place, and Illyrica with her silent wisdom. I loved the Poet, brother to me now, and the Angel. I loved Nora.

Come what may, I meant to keep them safe.

Chapter 30

———◆———

COLLISION

WE DID NOT KNOW HOW the Widow Brawnlyn had been at work. In truth, years would pass before we understood the whole of it. Nor did we truly understand the void left in the townspeople by plague and suffering. The Angel may have seen it more clearly than the rest of us did. Peacefully hiding together behind the Castle walls, we underestimated the power of hatred and the power of bitterness alike. But they found us.

Only two days had passed since our withdrawal from the world, and twilight had settled on the edges of the forest when I saw a slim figure, nervous, dressed in nondescript servant's clothing, trying to find a path. I watched him until I was sure he would enter the forest, and then slipped out of the trees and into his path. I folded my arms. It was more to my purpose to look intimidating than to be easily able to draw the sword at my side. He did not look like a threat.

"Why have you come here?" I demanded.

He was young, and hardly a brave soul—but there was something like truth in his expression. "Please," he quaked. "I come bearing a letter to the lady of the Castle."

I tilted my head. I wasn't sure who he could mean.

"To… to Nora," he said. "From my mistress, the young Lady Brawnlyn."

I held out my hand. "Give it to me," I said.

"Please," he stammered. "I was instructed…"

"No one passes through these woods now," I said. "I will take the letter. I give you my word it will be delivered before nightfall."

He licked his lips. "If my lady asks…"

"Tell her you surrendered her letter to the Hawk," I said.

His eyes were down on his own shoes. He stringently avoided my eyes. I watched him fumble in a pouch at his waist until he drew out a small roll of paper, tied with a dark purple ribbon. I recognized it—Genevieve often wore the colour. I held out my hand and he placed the roll in it, unhappily.

"Go your way," I said, hoping that he heard only strictness in my voice, and not anger. Whatever he heard, he was quick to obey. He turned on his heel and took himself gracelessly away.

I looked down at the roll in my hand. I almost wished I had not given my word. I had no desire to deliver the thing to Nora. I had not seen Genevieve in more than a year, and could hardly remember her face. She seemed to me more an idea than a person—an idea of darkness mocking beauty. As it was darkness I now stood guard against, I did not wish to bear it through the Castle doors. I knew that Nora cared for Genevieve somehow, and yet that they were antagonists in spirit. Sooner or later the light of the one would break the darkness of the other or be shrouded by it. I had been watching Nora. Every time she returned from Brawnlyn House I watched her. If ever I saw a sign that the darkness had touched her, had hurt her, I meant to pull her away. But it had not.

I carried the letter to her. She took it and read it quickly. A shadow passed over her face. I had been right, I thought, to wish the letter thrown away.

We were standing on the flagstones of the Castle's entrance. Nora had just finished lighting an oil lamp in the room before I entered. Its light flickered as a draft of warm summer air came through the door. She looked up at me and kept her voice low.

"There will be trouble," she said. "The Widow... I don't know what she's done; the letter is vague. But Genevieve summons me. Tonight."

"You won't go," I said. "No one is to leave here at night, you agreed on that."

"Hawk, this is not just a social call," Nora said. "I think she means to help us somehow."

"But that is not clear?" I said. "Perhaps she means to betray us."

There was a willfulness in the lines of Nora's mouth that I was not used to encountering. We had been long been equals but suddenly I remembered what it had been like to be an upstart boy under Nora's direction. It was the way she was looking at me— like a stubborn obstacle that needed to be moved out of the way. I grew a little desperate.

"Nora, you cannot!" I said.

"I have to," she answered.

And somehow, I knew she was right.

"Then let me escort you," I said.

She shook her head. "The Castle must be guarded. Both you and the Angel are needed. I'll be all right."

I couldn't help the words—they came without my bidding them. "As you were when last you went into the town?" I asked.

I saw the hurt flicker in the deep blue of her eyes, and then she smiled a little. "It is night, Hawk," she said. "No one will recognize me. And I do not mean to go into the town. Whatever else Genevieve does, she's hardly likely to stone me."

She had won the argument and I knew it. I was almost shocked when she engaged my eyes with her own and said, "Please let me go, Hawk."

I swallowed back a strange lump of emotion. "It's not my decision," I said.

She bowed her head. "It is," she said. "The Angel has given you that authority."

I nodded, hating myself. "Go, then," I said. "Do what you must."

She turned toward the door. Impulsively I reached out and touched her arm. She looked back at me, questioning. "Be careful," I said.

She smiled. My hand was still on her arm, and she reached up and took it gently, tightening her fingers around mine for a moment. "I will," she said. She dropped my hand and passed out through the door.

I watched her go for a moment, then ran and found the Pixie. I explained what had happened. Before she could protest I had gone out after Nora, determined to see her safely to the edge of the woods.

Twilight died into darkness. Night fell. There was no moon. The air was hot even now—almost stifling, I thought. The sounds of the forest groaned beneath the stillness of the air.

Hours passed, and Nora did not return. I began to grow weary and settled between the forked branches of a low tree.

How I slept I do not know, but I awoke to a sound. For a moment I thought it was Nora, but immediately I knew I was wrong. A small wind was blowing now, bringing with it the smell of oil and torch smoke. Footsteps tramped on the earth. Men were coming.

The townspeople—and more than the townspeople. I knew it as soon as I realized how many there were. The darkwood was crawling with them, bearing torches and swords and pitchforks, making their way inexorably to the Castle. Who the others were I did not know. Most likely they were in the hire of the Widow Brawnlyn. The townspeople were too blinded to understand that they were only doing the Widow's work. They thought— poor fools, they thought—that they were taking revenge for their own sakes.

I leaped up and sped through the woods, searching every favourite haunt for the Giant. If I could not find him quickly I meant to go straight to the Castle. The mob must not be allowed to reach the girls! My most precious charges, they were undefend- ed but for the Poet. But I did find him, easily. Most likely he was looking for me.

"There are hundreds," I gasped.

"A mob," he said. "They are looking for me."

"We can take shelter in the Castle," I said.

He looked at me. Only looked, but I understood him. We could not shelter in the Castle. We could not let the townspeople anywhere near it. Yet they were driving through the woods down so many different paths that we knew some were nearly there. We ran to meet them. On the edge of the lawn, we did. They seemed not to have faces. They were half-shrouded in darkness, lit in the torchlight like demonic things. Their voices rose up from them not as from men, but as from a single beast.

"The Giant! Take him! Take the man and slay him!"

The first men to rush forward were pushed back by the Giant's own staff, but others surrounded him. I charged into one, knocking him back, but others kept coming—and the Giant was no longer fighting. My sword was in my hand before I knew it was there, though I did not strike with it. I kept pushing men back with my fist and my head and the flat side of my sword. There were too many of them. I turned and saw that the Giant had been taken. They had bound his arms to his sides with long lengths of cord. In the torchlight he looked old, sad, and defeated.

Suddenly there was a shout. A man ran forward with a drawn sword, straight at the Giant. I dashed forward and met him. His sword met mine and went ringing away in a wild arc.

"No!" I shouted.

Another man, another sword. The blade slashed into my arm, through Nora's carefully laid bandages. I cried out. The pain was excruciating, as though my arm had taken a life of its own and was screaming. I gritted my teeth and managed to spit out, "No!" My breath came short and fast, but I fell in before the Giant, sword still in hand, daring the townspeople with my eyes to attack again. "Not without trial," I said, gasping away the pain as I spoke. "You will not kill a man without trial."

The Giant said nothing. There was some confusion in the crowd. They seemed to erupt in a brawl of their own—a fight not with swords but with words, and ideals. Some wanted him dead then and there; some recognized the truth in my words. Perhaps all they really wanted was to see him hung properly in the town square instead of butchered in the middle of the night. Whatever their motives, those who wished to put him on trial pushed their way through the crowd and grabbed onto the Giant's arms. They began to propel him away, through the woods.

Yet it was not over, for there were many—many—in the crowd possessed of a bloodier spirit. Perhaps the Widow had hired them to make sure our Angel died that night. Whatever the case, they tried, over and over, to reach him… to wound him… to kill him. And I drove them back. With stars of pain in my eyes, with my ears half-deafened, I drove them back. I heard myself shouting, over and over again, though I cannot tell what I said. More than once I believe I pleaded with those whose minds were saner. And over and over I met the enemy and fought them away.

What was the horror of that night to me? I cannot tell it. It was all a burning haze of struggle, pain, and desperation. Yet I kept them back. Whose was the strength with which I fought? It was not mine. Even now I am filled with gratitude when I think of it. A power kept us that night that had never belonged to me.

Sarah was standing in my room when the mob spilled out of the forest. From my window she saw the confrontation. She ran downstairs into the Pixie's arms and told her everything. It might have comforted me to know that they knew.

Somehow we reached the town. The pain in my arm, heightened by the continual battering of incensed foes, died away enough for me to gather my wits and call out, again and again, that the Giant must have a trial. That he would spend the night, not in a grave, but in a gaol. And somehow I won. There were men in the crowd who heard me and agreed. It was close to morning when I leaned my head against the stone wall of the gaol and closed my eyes, conscious that the Giant was breathing near me, sitting in a pile of straw behind bars.

I was too exhausted to worry for the Giant or for myself, but I could not sleep. I was too aware of one thing: that it had grown late in the woods before the mob came, and Nora had not returned.

Chapter 31

---·◆·---

THE VIGIL

THE NIGHT WORE ON in an uneasy truce. Some of the mob trickled away, but most stayed. They settled down for the night like an army laying siege, and I was the one-man army who kept them at bay. They had of course locked the iron door behind which the Giant now sat, as awake as I but silent. Even so, they kept their weapons ready to hand, half expecting some supernatural escape. If they expected it, we did not gratify them. Morning would come, and with it whatever monkey trial they cared to conduct. I had no wish to think beyond that.

I sat in the darkness with my hand resting on my sword. My eyes bored a hole in the stone wall across from me. The iron bars against my back were uncomfortable, but I preferred them to moving elsewhere. As long as I stayed with my back to the cell, no one could reach the Giant without encountering me. I thought of the Castle and wondered what they had seen or heard. I thought of Nora, hoping desperately that she had returned by now. My first fear, that Genevieve had betrayed her and she had walked into the Widow's trap, continually rose up and threatened to overwhelm me. I did not allow it. I could not afford to let myself feel desperation, no matter how desperate things in fact were.

Pain still seared my arm. I welcomed it. Pain was a distraction from the fears I did not want to face.

"Sparrowhawk."

I closed my eyes. The Giant's voice was home. In it was all the peace and mystery of the woodlands; the moonlit walls of the Castle and the flickering shadows of lamplight on the winding staircase leading to my room; changing seasons and the laughter of children. He did not sound afraid. He meant to comfort me. But how could I be comforted, when he and all he represented were so threatened?

"Sparrowhawk, look at me."

Reluctantly I shifted. I looked through the darkness at the great shadow that was his face. I could see his eyes, understanding and yet at peace. I said nothing.

"You must not allow yourself to be killed tomorrow," the Giant said. "Let them choose to do what they will. But you must go back to the Castle and take the girls away from this place."

I started to shake my head, but he continued. "Do you know the country three days east of here, where lies a forest greater than our own?"

I answered him. I did.

"There is a cave in the forest," the Giant said. "Underneath a great oak tree. Within, among the roots of the tree, there is gold. Enough to provide for them."

"Do not tell me this," I said. "It is your secret. You will live to return there."

I thought that he smiled, but I could not make out his features enough to know for sure. "You will be a magnificent protector to them, Hawk. You have grown worthy."

"Only because of you," I choked out. His next words brought tears to my eyes. In the darkness I cried and was not ashamed.

"Take care of Nora," he said. "If she does not yet return your love, she will. Watch over her, Hawk; there is none like her in the world. She was my first treasure, and still perhaps most precious to me."

I could not answer him. I only turned my back again and sobbed like a child.

My tears had not had time to dry when I heard a sound without. I stood and went to the window, where I could look out on the waiting mob. The outside of the gaol was lit sparingly by a few torches, casting an orange light over those who slept and those who watched. And there I beheld a marvelous sight.

The children were threading their way through the crowd, quietly, solemnly, picking their way over the arms and legs of men who had sprawled out on the paving stones. Those who awoke to see them exclaimed at them—the noise I had heard—but could hardly gather their wits enough to stop them. What can men do against such an invasion? Little girls in summer dresses, some holding hands, two clinging tightly to the Pixie, who was leading them through the crowd, and another two to Illyrica, who stood at the rear and made sure the stragglers were not forgotten. The Poet stood behind her, little more than a shadow beyond the torchlight.

Every one of the children was there: above forty, like flowers washed over the camp by some mystic wave. The Pixie led them up to the door and opened it. One by one they tumbled in. A few ran to me and threw their arms around me. Before I could compose myself they were wiping the tears off of my face with the palms of their warm little hands.

The others went past me and slipped through the iron bars without hindrance. They settled themselves in around the Giant:

on his shoulders, in the crooks of his arms, on his lap, under his coat, laying with their heads on his knees and ankles. The cell, made for much more hardened criminals, was just big enough to contain them all. Sarah was one of the last in. She paused and looked back at me with her old, strange, too serious eyes. I shook my head in wonder. She smiled a little and slipped the rest of the way through.

A moment later Illyrica was bandaging my arm back up with strips of cloth torn from her own skirt. I had hardly known she was there. The Pixie stood against the bars of the cell and folded her arms, looking at the still-open door of the gaol as though daring the mob to come in and face her. And then there was the Poet, stomping his boots clean of mud in the doorway. He knelt by the cell door and filed away at the bars with an iron tool. He handed me another. I knelt beside him and went to work. It was not to let the Giant out. We knew he could not get past the mob outside. It was to let us in. This night we would be together. One family.

But Nora was not there. The Pixie told me in a whisper— too hushed, because she did not want anyone to hear—that Nora had not returned to the Castle, nor had there been any word of her. It was wrong that we should hold our vigil without her, but we had no choice.

Chapter 32

———◆———

GENEVIEVE

NORA HAD GONE QUICKLY at Genevieve's summons. She was sure the widow's daughter meant to help, and surely, if we had ever needed help, it was now. It was dark when she arrived at Brawnlyn House, and she had slipped in a back way. A servant's door had been left unlocked. Nora had used it before when visiting Genevieve, and the Widow knew nothing of it.

The house was dark, as it always was. The Widow lit no lights except where absolutely necessary. She was a creature of darkness and liked to dwell in it. In her own chambers there was seldom lit more than a single, twisted candle. But it was not to the Widow that Nora made her way, up a flight of stairs, feeling her way through the gloomiest parts of the house. At last she reached an old, old room where she was sure she would find Genevieve waiting. It had been a library once, but a fire had destroyed half of it, and it had never been repaired. It was high in the house. Part of the roof gaped open and let in the summer air. Nora stepped into the room. Starlight shone down through the open places. There was no other light. The blackened walls with their ruined books seemed a menacing presence.

She stood, a little winded by the speed of her trip, unsure what to do next. She had no wish to alert the Widow of her presence, but did not know how to find Genevieve without causing a stir. And then, suddenly enough to make her gasp, there came the sound of a match. A candle flared to life behind her. She whirled around. Genevieve was there.

For a moment they stood without speaking. Genevieve was not looking at Nora. Her face was turned up to the ruined roof, eyes on the stars. She looked down abruptly and said, "Thank you for coming."

It was not a humble thanks. Genevieve could not speak without haughtiness. She held herself so much in contempt that she only knew how to scorn others.

"Why did you call me here?" Nora asked.

"There will be trouble." Genevieve cut herself off, then began again. "My mother has been… I heard about what happened to you in the village. I'm sorry."

Nora took a step closer to the widow's daughter. Her hand went to the bruise on her neck—as it often did. It was not a gesture she thought about. But it drew Genevieve's eyes to the mark. She flinched at the sight.

"It was not your fault," Nora said.

"It was my mother's," Genevieve said. "She has been poisoning the people. She…"

"You needn't speak of her," Nora said. "It can only hurt you… she is your mother."

"I hate her," Genevieve said.

Nora drew a deep breath. "You called me here for a reason. Only to tell me that there will be trouble? We knew. We have been preparing."

Genevieve waved her hand, dismissing Nora's words. "Yes, yes," she said. "You have not prepared enough. You should have left. All of you should have left."

"Is it too late?" Nora said.

Genevieve met her eyes suddenly. "I hope not," she said. There was more conviction in those words than in anything Genevieve had ever said before. "But if… if you cannot leave in time…" She seemed to be in distress, almost in pain. Whatever she had to say would not come easily. It was forced out, past her pride and her fears and her carefully frozen heart.

Nora went to her side and laid a gentle hand on her arm. "It's all right," she said.

They were interrupted by the sudden arrival of a servant. From Nora's description of him, I know it was the same young man who I had met in the woods. He was less nervous here, but still touched with cowardice, and very unhappy.

"It is too late, my lady," he said. "A mob has gone into the forest. They will kill the Giant, they say."

Nora let out a cry. Genevieve grabbed her arm with a vice grip. "Did you follow them?" she demanded.

"Yes," the servant said. "They were met by the Giant, who looks very terrible but will not fight them it seems, and the one called Hawk—I think they must kill him, for when I left he was fighting like a madman."

Nora tore herself away and ran toward the door, but Genevieve was faster. She reached the door first, shoving her servant out ahead of her, and pulled it shut behind her. There was a sickening click as she locked it.

Part of the wall near the doorframe had rotted away, and Nora could see Genevieve without, pale and terrible. She held the key in her shaking hand.

"Genevieve, let me out!" Nora pleaded.

Genevieve shook her head and tightened her fingers around the key. "You can do nothing *now*," she said. "One can only stop a mob who possesses greater force than they, and you do not."

Her words were almost contemptuous. Nora leaned against the door and fought back desperate tears. She pushed against it, but it would not move. Her eyes went to the rotted place, but Genevieve anticipated her. "You cannot tear the wall apart. There's brick beneath it. And I would call for mother. She would not let you leave."

Nora moved away from the door and ran to the window across the library, looking out across the sleeping fields and woods as though she could find us with her eyes. She turned back again. "If I can do nothing," she said, "I would rather die with them than stay here!"

Genevieve took a step back and shook her beautiful head. "But you can't," she said. "You mustn't."

Tears were running down Nora's face now. She lifted her hands, pleading. "You will let me lose everything I love without even trying to help them?" she said.

"I will not let you die," Genevieve answered. "The people say you're a child-stealer, a murderess. Mother feeds the lies. They'll kill you too if you go. But I won't let you go. I won't let them kill you."

She left the hall. Nora sank down against the door and lifted her eyes to the stars, praying in the blackness of despair. Her torture was worse than mine, for I knew the reality of all that was happening, and she was left to the mercy of imagination. I had the hope of dying with the Giant; she faced the spectre of surviving alone. She was torn with worry for the children; stabbed by near-panic for the Angel—and for me.

And then, with morning not far off, Genevieve appeared again, unlocked the door, and pulled Nora to her feet. She handed her a small bundle of papers. "They are not dead," she said. "They are in the gaol, in the town. There will be a trial in the morning. Take these. They may be enough to save you all."

Nora took the papers slowly. She looked at Genevieve with all her questions in her eyes.

"Do as you must," Genevieve said. "Only do not ruin me lightly."

With these enigmatic words she stood aside, leaving Nora the open door. Within minutes Nora had flown down the stairs to the stables, where she picked a horse, mounted it without bothering with a saddle, and tore across the fields toward the town.

Chapter 33

---◆◆◆---

BEFORE THE MOB

NORA ARRIVED JUST AS THE earliest light was seeping into the morning air. The mob encamped without the gaol had hardly begun to stir. The pounding hooves of Nora's horse woke many of them to the fact that day was breaking. I was on my feet the instant I heard the horse approaching. My heart leaped when I saw who rode it. She charged through the center of the mob and dismounted at the door, her hair loose and windblown. There was a confused clamour of voices as some of the men recognized her. She had been villainized along with the Giant, and I saw one man start forward as though he would lay hands on her. He thought better of it—perhaps he realized that it was to their purposes that Nora was going *into* the gaol—and slumped back down.

Her hands were shaking as she came through the door. Awash with adrenaline and the aftermath of that awful night, afraid of what she might find when she stepped into the gaol, she was more beautiful than ever. She looked on the gathering in the little cell: children slowly waking, blinking up at her, the Giant welcoming her from the bottom of the loving heap with his dark, gentle eyes. She bowed her head as strong emotion swept over her.

My voice had caught in my throat and seemed to be going through convulsions. I could only stand there like a fool.

The Pixie spoke first: "Nora," she said. A sob almost escaped her.

Nora rushed to her, into the cell, and the whole family embraced her at once. I stood without, still at the window where I had gone to see her approach. To my amazement, she pulled herself away from the children and sought me out. She rushed over to where I stood. Her eyes brushed past the window and the crowd that waited without, lit now by the coming dawn and a few still-smoking torches. I saw the troubled expression on her face, and it smote me. I found my voice.

"We will beat them yet," I said.

"We will," she said, looking back at me. Her voice dropped to a barely audible whisper. "Genevieve has helped us."

With those words she pulled a small packet of papers, tied with twine, from a pocket in her skirt. She handed it to me without a word and watched while I slowly untied it.

I didn't have time to finish. The door burst open. Men spilled in, gruff and dirty, looking like they had spent the night in as much comfort as we had. They had come to drag their prisoners out to trial. But they seemed different somehow, more subdued. As they stepped over the little ones, ordered Illyrica and the Pixie to stand aside, and commanded the Poet not to try anything, they seemed almost embarrassed. But I knew they were not ashamed enough. One man stood at the door, calling orders.

"Clear them out!" he commanded. "Take the Giant!"

He turned his eyes to the corner by the window. He pointed in Nora's direction with his chin. "Her too."

I tensed to stop them, even as the Pixie and the Poet both decided to disobey orders and try something in the cell. A voice boomed through the gaol and put an end to all of our bravado.

"Peace, all of you!" It was the Giant.

I fell back and let the men take Nora. She smiled at me encouragingly as they pushed her out the door just before the Giant. He also looked back at me, and I understood the look. The papers in my hand. It was up to me to make use of them. It was the hardest job Nora and the Giant could have left me with—at that moment I would rather have done anything than read!

The Pixie led the charge out the door after the men, Katie in her arms, children in tow. She was flushed and determined. I was left alone in the gaol to try and concentrate enough to make the ink jots on the paper form themselves into words. When they did, I willed the words to mean something. Anything! How could any man read when every nerve was straining to act?

Outside, the "trial" had begun. They had elected men to judge. The wainwright, bereaved father, stood at the head of them. I caught sight of his face through the window and felt plunged in despair again. There was a veritable blackness in his countenance that was horrible to behold; anger and hatred I could not imagine. He seemed hardly to see the children. All he could see was the Giant, the man he believed had taken his son from him. I remembered the way he had come to meet us when we bore the body home to him. I wondered if he was seeing the scene again, too. I could not blame him for his bitterness.

A wooden platform stood near the gaol. I thought it might be the remains of an old gallows. The Giant was taken up on it, though he already stood head, shoulders, and chest above the others in the crowd. The judges climbed up after him, and the accusations began. Nora stood beneath the platform, a guard on either side. I saw her turn and look at me with urgency in her eyes. The papers. I wasn't reading the papers. I tore my attention from the trial and tried again to understand what I was looking at.

The accusation cut the air. "Thief… stealer of children!"

The Pixie's voice rang out in response. She had pushed her way to the front of the crowd and was looking up at the wainwright now, daring him to respond to the passion in her eyes. "He did," she said. "From a ditch… from death, he stole me. And the others! He took us in when plague and poverty killed our parents. Where is the crime in that?"

She could not be ignored. The wainwright looked down at her angrily, but the sea of small faces that peered back up at him caught him off guard. The Pixie was formidable enough on her own. As general of a small army, armed with innocence, she was more than his match.

His voice had softened a little when he spoke. "Get these children out of here," he said. "They should not have to witness this."

"To witness the condemnation of a good and innocent man?" It was the Poet who answered now, stepping forward with a grave expression on his face. "Then they should not have to live—not in this world. Think, man: what are you doing?"

"My son is dead," the wainwright choked. "Where is justice for me?"

"The Giant did not kill your son," the Poet said. "Not one of us did. He fell and… it was an accident."

The wainwright spoke through clenched teeth, as though he would ward off the truth and the revelation of his own wrong-doing. "We heard reports," he said. "There was a battle. You drew the sword on my son; you struck him with arrows!"

Sarah stepped forward and said in a very small voice, "That was me."

The wainwright stopped short. He had expected to convict a

Giant, not to uncover the guilt of a small girl. He looked down at her and blinked. "What?" he said.

"I shot the arrow," she said. "Your son attacked us. He was leading a band of thieves. We were only trying to take care of each other. We didn't mean for him to die!"

Illyrica put her arm around Sarah's shoulders as she began to shake. In a moment she was crying, and the old, deadened Sarah vanished in a flood of tears. Illyrica pulled her close and stroked her hair. She looked up at the wainwright with her eloquent eyes. He seemed to be coming apart. Anger, hatred, and lies had nearly driven him to murder, but they weren't protection enough against this. Could anything be?

He wheeled on the Giant. "You," he spat. "You did not speak. You did not tell us…" In an instant, the wainwright's struggle was over. He heard the absurdity of his own accusation. The Giant had been given no chance to speak—and if he had, should he have turned such as Sarah and Illyrica over to the mob? They had as much responsibility for the boy's death as he.

He bowed his head, a grieving, broken father. The vengeful spirit that had driven him was gone.

I hardly noticed. For while the trial's strange progression was unfolding, Genevieve's papers had begun to speak to me—and the story they told was so strange, so fascinating, so *condemning*, that I knew it had the power to change our world forever.

I had not learned it too soon. The wainwright's surrender was hardly accomplished when there came a clatter of horses and coach wheels. The true magisterial power of the province arrived like a dark cloud of wrath. No tears or truth could sway the judgment now. The mob would have blood yet. The Widow Brawnlyn had come.

Chapter 34

POWER IN PAPERS

LIKE AN EMPRESS THE WIDOW descended from her coach, casting her disdainful eye over the crowd. She saw in an instant what had happened. The wainwright had been swayed; her cause almost lost. But the power that had caught the attention of the mob—innocence and loyalty—had no more effect on the Widow's eye than the power of truth had on her heart. I saw with troubled understanding that the crowd would listen to her. Their ears were accustomed to her poison. They fed on it. Already they seemed ready to bend.

The Widow gathered her black skirts and climbed the steps to the old ruined gallows. She passed a look of scorn on the Pixie and her little ones, and another on Nora, and then turned her narrowed eyes on the Giant. She said something to him, but I could not hear. I was already out the door, pushing my way through the crowd, shouting for them to part.

Just as I reached the wooden steps, I saw the Giant open his palm and show something to the Widow. She blanched. Somehow, the Giant had struck a blow—but I had no time to reflect on what had happened, for I had a blow of my own to give.

"Lady Brawnlyn," I said, my voice low. She whirled around, nearly brushing against me in the small space of the platform.

She was livid. She had not yet had time to speak to the crowd, to raise arms against us—she had not expected us to confront her so boldly.

The open hatred in her eyes as she took in the sight of me did not disturb me in the slightest. I smiled at her. "My lady," I said. "I suggest that you step down and speak with me."

"You have nothing to say to me," the Widow spat. "And I will not waste words on you."

I raised my voice a little so that some of the crowd could hear me. "Shall we speak here, then?" I asked. "I have a contract to discuss with you: a contract made with one Thomas Breward, leader of…"

"Hush, boy," she said. Her voice was harsh as she grated out the words. Her tone lunged at me. If she could have stopped me physically, she would have. "I will speak with you."

"Good," I said, loudly enough for everyone to hear. I gestured to the path I had made through the crowd, all the way back to the door of the gaol. "Shall we?"

Raising her chin in the air, she once again gathered her skirts and made her way down the steps. I looked up at the Giant. "Will you come?" I asked.

He shook his head slowly, a faint smile playing at his mouth. "No," he said. "You can do this without me."

I took Nora's arm as I passed her. Somehow it seemed that she should be with me. Together we followed the Widow through the door of the gaol, and I turned and gently latched it behind me.

The Widow wasted no time. "What do you know of Thomas Breward?" she demanded.

"That he has paid you over two thousand pounds in tribute in the last four years," I said. "And that lately, as your people have suffered famine and hardship, your coffers have only grown deeper."

Nora folded her arms and leaned back against the door. The deep satisfaction on her face was evident.

The Widow gathered the folds of her shawl around her. "What if they have?" she asked. "There is no law against tribute."

"There is," I said, "when it comes of money stolen from your people. Thomas Breward oversees the bands of robbers who so unfortunately plague your country."

She pursed her lips. "You cannot prove that."

"Can't we?" I asked. "We know it. How do we know it, if we have no proof?"

Her face twisted. "Your leader is a demon."

"You once told me," I said, "that this province was haunted by legendary villains. I now know that there is only one such ghost. Shall we reveal her to the people?"

"You wouldn't dare," the Widow said.

Nora pushed herself away from the wall and stepped forward. She looked the Widow steadfastly in the eye. "You have money," she said. "And your people need help. Help them. Be the ruler you ought to be. For the sake of your daughter, who you have used so shamelessly. For the sake of your future. Do away with the villain yourself, and we will not have to."

"You little minx," the Widow spat. Nora only continued to look steadily at her until the Widow turned her back.

"I'll do it," she said.

"Banish the thieves," I said. "If they strike again, and what they take is not repaid within the week, we will come to you for it."

She nodded—still not looking at us.

"Do not think that you can save yourself by striking against us again," I continued. "We have proof. We will distribute it well enough."

She turned icily. "Have you any more demands?"

Nora shook her head. "No," she said.

"Then I will take my leave," the Widow said. She went to the door and yanked it open. A huge frame blocked her way.

The Giant ducked inside and smiled at us. "Are you finished, children?" he asked.

I smiled. "Yes."

"Then I have a threat of my own to make," the Giant said. He looked down at the Widow. His eyes narrowed. There in the door of the gaol I saw again the powerful man who had confronted me in the woods long ago, half-hidden in shadow, terrifying in his strength. "You saw what I held out to you?" he asked.

"I did," she answered. She seemed hardly able to get the words out. Anger gripped her tongue.

"Then you know the power I hold over you," he said. "I do not now choose to use it. Keep the terms set for you by my son and by my daughter. Keep them, or know that I will remove from you everything you now hold dear."

In answer, the Widow stormed past him, entered her coach, and drove away in a cloud of dust.

The door swung open behind her. Beyond it, the wainwright approached with his hat in his hand. He looked a sad and defeated man. The Pixie and the others had made their way to the door as well. They now stood waiting for us, and watching.

"I'm sorry," the wainwright began.

The Giant laid a hand on his shoulder. "As am I," he said. "What you have lost no one can repay."

One of the children slipped away from the Pixie and took the wainwright's hand. She looked up at him with big eyes, and he smiled down at her. His own eyes were full of tears.

At a nod from me, Nora took the papers from my hand and gave them to the wainwright. We alone knew what they were—contracts, correspondence, records of financial transactions for the past ten years. Every one condemned the Widow. She had been leeching off of her own people by way of robbery and terror for a long time, hidden behind the masks of bandits and the faces of thieves. But we also knew that to depose the Widow would mean trouble for the province: legal trouble, greater impoverishment. And it would destroy Genevieve.

"These are not to be read," Nora said. "Take them, and distribute them among men you trust."

"If ever you find yourselves under the heel of thieves again, read them," I said. "Only then."

The wainwright nodded. "I understand, young man. And I thank you."

I swallowed a lump in my throat and looked up at the Giant. Suddenly relief was flooding every part of me. I smiled up at him as I had never, never smiled before. He looked down at me and smiled in return.

"Lead the way, Hawk," he said. "It is time to go home."

Chapter 35

——◆——

HOME

HAPPY ENDINGS, I AM TOLD, are not really to be expected in the world. Indeed, it seemed against all the laws of nature that we should have won out over the Widow Brawnlyn. But there was a higher law watching over us: a happy, merciful law, a law invoked in births and spring and resurrections. Even now, I can't describe how I felt as we broke out of the woods, all of us together, hand-in-hand with the whole tribe of little ones, to see the white walls of the Castle cheerfully sparkling in the sun—just for us. I could hear the creek running, and I felt the anticipation of pulling the boat back out of its hiding place in the old cellar. A breeze was playing in the treetops. It was singing the same song that leaped up over and over again in my heart: *Saved!*

We were saved… rescued… so many threads had come together, against all odds, to form our homecoming. We were saved by Nora's compassion, by the Pixie's wits, by the human heart that against all odds dwelt in Genevieve Brawnlyn. Saved by the Giant's innocence, his goodness. Saved by the Widow's guilt. Saved by all the nights in the woods, long ago, when the Giant had taught me to fight and to persevere and to care about what was right. Without his training I could never have stood against the marauders when they came.

I told Nora as much that night, as we sat by the open door of the kitchen, looking out at the stars. The only light in the room came from a candle on the table and the embers of supper that still burned in the belly of the cookstove and leaked out around the edges of the stove's iron door. She smiled at me as I talked, all of my wonder overflowing in words.

"And by you, Hawk," she said, finishing my list. "You were a hero."

A cool wind blew in from the woods. I looked out into the darkness. I could feel the colour in my face. I hoped she couldn't see it. The door of the kitchen was wide, and we sat opposite each other with our backs to the solid wooden frame. When I looked back at her, she had turned her eyes up to the stars. Her hair was long, flowing over her shoulders and stirring slightly in the breeze; its deep gold highlights called forth by the flickering of the candle. Her face was serene in the starlight. She smiled and looked down at me with a suddenness that took my breath away.

"Thank you," she said.

Early that fall, the Giant had his first attack.

We didn't understand quite what was happening to him, but he seemed almost to be expecting it. We made him a bed in the soft room. There he lay, ashen-faced and weak, while Nora and the Pixie tended him and I took his place in the woods. I had added furring to my list of duties. Though I knew the Giant to possess a great treasure, it was still his desire that we support ourselves from the land around the Castle. Whenever I could, I came in to see him. I would sit by him for half an hour here, an hour there.

He regained some of his strength and returned to the woods, but he seemed to have aged ten years. I realized with a sinking feeling that though we had averted death in the town, it could not be kept at bay forever. He had a second spell in the winter, worse than the first, but once again he recovered and returned to his old ways.

In the spring, he called me to his side. He was well then; almost as strong, it seemed, as he had been when first he came across me trespassing on his lands. I thought he wanted to speak to me about the furs, or some repairs that were needed on the Castle. I went to him as soon as he called and found him sitting on a fallen log in a mossy clearing that he had always loved. He looked up at me when I approached and smiled with a twinkle in his dark eyes.

He reached for me and placed his hand on my shoulder. I placed mine on his. It was a tender gesture: father to son.

"Hawk," the Giant said, "I am going to send you away."

I tensed and nearly pulled my arm away. He chuckled. "Easy," he said. "Not forever. I have some business I want you to attend to in another province." He named the province and the city. I knew of it. He then named a lawyer, and I looked at him with a frown. I could not imagine what business he could have in a place as distant from his woodland realm as a lawyer's office.

"I told you, in the gaol, that I possess something of a fortune," the Giant said. "It is mine legally."

I turned a little red. "I didn't think it wasn't…"

"But you did not imagine that I might use lawyers to administer it?" He took his hand away and looked down at his deeply worn hands with a half-smile. "I have not always been the man I am now. I want you to go, Hawk, because I am giving the treasure away. I have written a will, and I want you to take it to the city."

I opened my mouth and searched for words, but he did not wait for me to find them. "I am giving the bulk of the treasure to you," he said. "And all that goes with it. I am rich in daughters, but you are the only son I have ever had. I have given you all I can, and I am content that you have become a true man. If you'll have them, I want to leave the Castle, and all its inhabitants, in your care when I go."

I nodded and found a few words at last, though I could hardly put them coherently together. "I would not have it any other way."

"Good," the Giant said. He stood and clapped me on the shoulder again. "Leave as soon as you can." He looked up at the sky, which was beautiful and clear: unusually so for spring. "Today, if possible."

He took a parchment from his shirt, and gave it to me. It was his will.

In something of a daze, I returned to the Castle. Nora was nowhere to be found, nor was the Pixie, so I went to work packing up enough things to keep me clothed for the entire trip and fed for the first few days. When I was finished, I bound it all up in a bundle and hefted it up on my back. I made my way out the door and halfway across the lawn, looking everywhere for those to whom I had to say good-bye. Nora found me before I found her. I heard her calling across the lawn and saw her running toward me. She stopped close by me, out of breath.

"Isabelle said you are leaving," she said. I heard the question in her voice and a note of warning, but I did not entirely comprehend her tone. More the fool I. I was so wrapped up in my own questions that I failed to realize what Isabelle had actually told Nora.

"Yes," I said.

"Where will you go?" she asked. "I thought…"

I told her the name of the town. She looked at me piercingly, her blue eyes searching my puzzled face.

"I hope that whatever takes you there is well worth leaving us," she said, quietly. All of a sudden I realized what she thought.

"I should hope so," I said, "as the Giant is sending me; but Nora, I will come back."

A change came over her face that altered her so greatly it made something inside me knot up. I saw relief in her face— joy— very great depth of feeling. And my stomach continued to knot, because there was something I had long wanted to ask her, and dreaded to—but now, for the first time, I knew that she loved me. I looked up to the walls of the Castle, gleaming behind her, and the green depths of the woods behind. Everything paled in comparison with her beauty. I swallowed hard.

"I will return," I said. "As quickly as I can, in about… about a month. I would not *leave*."

"I didn't think you would," she said, not meeting my eyes. "Forgive me, Hawk: I feared…"

"Don't fear," I said. "I love this place. I mean to stay forever. To take care of things when… when I'm needed."

"You're needed now," Nora said. She looked up at me and smiled. "I can't imagine this place without you."

I drew in a deep breath and said, "Nora, will you marry me when I come back?"

She blushed, but did not turn her eyes away. She held out her hand to me. I took it, and she rose up on her toes a little and kissed my cheek.

"Of course," she said.

"I love you," I told her.

"I know," she said. "And I you."

I grinned and turned to go, feeling a thousand feet taller and a thousand times stronger and a thousand years happier than I had a moment ago.

"Hawk!" she called. I turned back. My heart thrilled to her smile… radiant, beautiful joy. "Come back soon," she said.

Chapter 36

PARADISE DEEPENS

TRUE TO MY ESTIMATION, my business in the city took about a month. Every step of the way there I longed to be already heading back, back to the forest and the children and the woman I loved, back to my heart's father, back to the white walls of the best and dearest Castle in the world. Once I had arrived, my business with the lawyers absorbed me enough to alleviate some of my suffering. I found that the Giant had done more than simply leave me a fortune. Nor was he making idle talk when he called me "son." He had adopted me. Me, Nora, the Pixie, and every last child in the Castle. To each of us he had left an inheritance. To Nora and me he gave the guardianship of the children—all except for little Kate, who was legally given to the Pixie's care.

Along with his fortune—and, I reflected, his real treasure—he passed along the mystery of his past to me. In the town I learned at last where the Giant had come from, where his gold had been obtained, why he held power over the Widow Brawnlyn. I had not imagined it for a moment, and once I had learned all there was to learn, I kept it close to myself.

I returned to the Castle in the summer and found that the Giant had once again fallen ill. This time, he was very weak. The Pixie gave up shooing the children out of his room at the Giant's request, and they spent all of their time clustered around him: reading to him, singing little made-up songs, petting his old weathered face and hands. Illyrica all but moved in to the Castle. She spent every moment at the foot of the bed, silently watching, memorizing his face. The Poet was there every moment he was not working, and Nora and I gave up most of our usual responsibilities to be there as well. He wanted us there. And somehow, the old threats that had kept one of us patrolling the woods every day for so long seemed far away—without power to touch us.

The night after my return I went into the room. There was no fire in the hearth—the heat of summer made it unnecessary—but a lantern near the bed was lit. Illyrica was asleep at the foot of it. I passed her quietly and looked down on my old friend. I thought he was asleep, but he looked up after a moment and smiled.

"Sit down, boy," he said.

There was a chair beside the bed, so I did.

"You know more about me now than any living person," the Giant said. "Except the lawyers, and I'm not sure they are living persons."

I laughed, quietly so as not to awaken Illyrica. "I don't understand you," I told him. "But I hope to… one day."

The Giant nodded. "Nora told me that you want to marry her."

"Very much," I said.

His voice was faint when he answered. "No delays, then," he said. "There is no reason to heap up time in your way."

I heard what he meant. We hadn't much time left. We both knew it. I had tried to say the same to Nora earlier, but she had not wanted to hear me. I understood.

The very next morning I told Nora that we would wed as soon as she had a dress ready. She went to work immediately. The Pixie cast every window in the Castle open to air everything out. The children picked flowers of every colour imaginable— with a greater abundance of pinks and purples than I had known existed—and arranged them in every corner and on every surface in the place. The Castle seemed to have filled itself with the seasons and blossomed forth in glory. I went into town and traded an armload of fox-furs for a good set of clothes, and when I came home it was to the sight of a wooden chest that had just been delivered to the Castle: a gift from Genevieve Brawnlyn. Open, it yielded yards upon yards of sheer cloth, white flecked with gold. Illyrica snatched it up, and I saw no more of it.

The day came. The Giant could not get out of his bed, so we held the wedding inside. I was shoved up the stairs the night before and not allowed to come down until the women and girls had arranged everything to their satisfaction. Then, dressed and groomed as best as I could, I came down the stairs and pushed open the doors to the soft room.

I stepped into an elven hall. Genevieve's cloth formed a canopy over the whole room and came down in an archway at the end of the aisle. The Pixie seemed to have moved half the forest into the room: the whole thing was green and growing. Mossy branches and green flowering vines seemed to have sprung spontaneously to joy over us. Vines twisted down the archway, blooming with small roses.

We would say our vows at the foot of the Giant's bed. The Giant himself was sitting up, smiling broadly, looking healthier and happier than I had seen him in some time. His clothes were simple buckskin dyed deep grey, trimmed with fur. They were also new. Illyrica had been at work. His eyes summoned me, and

I went to his side. He looked up at me and nodded, satisfied with what he saw.

And then he looked past me, and I turned to see what he did. Nora had entered the room.

She wore a long gown of white. Blue threads, royal like her eyes, embroidered her neckline and the hem of the skirt that flowed over her bare feet. Her hair was long, with strands of blue flowers braided through it. She was a swan coming across the water: faerie queen, entering the world of mortals. How my heart welled up as she came. My sister, my wife. We had worked side by side in quiet times; been companions in arms in times of war. She was to me the daughter of peace, promise of beauty, earnest of life. She was the reward I had once thought to earn, but now knew to be far too precious for the earning. She could only be what she was—a gift of grace. With her to stand beside me I could stand against any nightmare; bear any loss; defeat any foe.

Though I trembled within, when I held out my hands to her they were steady. She took them and looked up at me. We were lost in each other's eyes. I could hardly hear the words the Giant spoke. We pledged to each other our faithfulness, our care, our love; she obedience, I that, were it in my power, she would never regret that she had me to obey. The little girls around us leaned forward and drank in every word. The Giant, the Pixie, and the Poet cried.

The moment came. I folded her in my arms and kissed her.

I had never imagined how sweetly paradise could deepen.

Chapter 37

THE GENTLE FALLING OF WINTER

THE GIANT DID RISE FROM the sickbed after Nora and I were married at his feet. He lived to wander the woods he so loved again. But the end could not be staved off forever. Two years later, in the dawn of a blue-white winter, our Angel left us.

We buried him wrapped in furs and laid to rest in a great pine box, which the Poet and I had made together and Sarah had helped to sand. His going had not been unexpected—at least, he seemed to expect it. A man ever of few words, he yet found time to pull each of us aside and speak words of love and of wisdom. Though most of us never told any other soul what he had said, I think that even little Kate has never forgotten what she heard from his mouth.

Evening fell on the day of his burial, and I had not yet left the graveside. I stayed by it, under the trees at the bottom of the lawn, all through the night. Moon and stars shone down on me through the bare branches, recalling nights of training in the forest, and other nights, of fear, of humiliation, of growth. Since I had gone to settle his affairs for him, I alone knew what he had sacrificed to follow the narrow path he had chosen through life— but perhaps, as I had taken his position as father and guardian, I alone knew what he had gained. Through the cold chill of the night I sat and promised him, with words, tears, and stillness, that I would not fail in the charge he had given me. Nora came at dawn and curled up beside me with her head on my shoulder, and together we sat until morning was well on its way. Then we arose and went to our duties.

How word of the Giant's death reached the nearby towns I do not know, but it did; and before long a slow trickle of visitors began. They came, laid tokens on the grave, and told us with solemn faces how sorry they were. It was the beginning of a new day for us. The long coldness between us and the outside world was beginning to thaw, and while I intended that we would always remain apart, I saw in the faces of the townspeople the faces of those who might become friends.

The wainwright came and shed tears by the grave. He shook my hand and Nora's, and looked over the little ones who had gathered around us. He seemed so drawn to stay that Nora invited him to dinner, and he came—not for the last time. The children surrounded him at dinner, plied him with questions, and made him smile beneath his weary brow. Nora and I looked at each other when we saw the smile. We understood one another perfectly. We meant to make the wainwright quite at home in the Castle.

Of all who mourned the Angel's passing, none did so more deeply or with more quietude than Nora. His first child—his co-rescuer—heart that understood his perfectly. She faced his passing with a courage I could only admire, but when she grew weak and childlike in her memories and grief, it was mine to hold her and give her comfort—and by some miracle, she was comforted.

In that same winter, Sarah and I turned the old cellar into a woodshop, and as I was not so busy in the woods in the season of snow, we at last finished the boat. It would wait for the river to run again before it sailed, but it stood to us, brave little ship, like a symbol of the future.

Chapter 38

———◆———

ALL THINGS WELL

THE ANGEL'S DEATH LEFT US all with an emptiness inside, a poverty that made us feel how fragile our lives were. But life grew rich again: rich beyond my imagining. It grew richer in every child added to the Castle's treasure-store—children who called me "Father" and nursed at Nora's breast; other children who sat on the Poet's knee and grew to know the virtue of an overflowing silence as they knew it in their mother. Children who came, as they had in the past, from broken carriages and empty hearths, from danger and poverty and illness, to pour upon us their laughter and their love. It grew richer in the forest, as it grew older and greener, and yielded more of its secrets to us with every passing year. It grew richer in the children who grew up, in the girls who became women: in Sarah who went back to our old home by the sea and started an orphanage there—a Castle all her own, full of her spunk and courage and love; in Isabelle who married a young nephew of the old wainwright and made him the dearest wife who ever lived; in Kate who became a beauty and learned how to tell stories. It grew richer: rich beyond all imagining or desire.

The Pixie never married. She lived always in the Castle with us, until Kate entered womanhood and I began scaring suitors away, and even after Kate went away on the arm of one who loved her as I loved Nora. Still, though years passed, the Pixie seemed haunted by a memory of girlhood: splendid in mystery and innocence. She who had so wished for independence from the Castle seemed least able to leave it. But I would not have you think her a sad or tragic figure. While the Pixie lived, yesterday lived still— joyous, beautiful yesterday, weaving itself into the present with every word, every touch, every radiant smile the Pixie bestowed. She was the personification of all we had once had, and while we had her, we could lose nothing.

Four months after the Giant's passing, Genevieve Brawnlyn came to us, dressed in black. Her mother had taken ill suddenly and died with a curse on her lips. Genevieve had wept for the first time in her life, for everything that was broken in her, and then she came to us for healing. Nora loved her and covered her with affection, and the children made her laugh and put new joy into her eyes. The strange and stormy young woman I had once imagined I might love slowly melted into someone capable of loving in return.

She ruled over the province alone. More than one man came to seek her hand, but she turned every one away. When she needed advice, she came to us for it, and sometimes to the wainwright, who was often at our table. I never told Genevieve what I knew of the Giant's past, and of my own position in her land, but I somehow knew that she knew. I could see it in her eyes. Sometimes she hinted at it. She knew that her mother had not been the rightful ruler of the province at all: that her father's brother had fathered a son who inherited the family treasure and disappeared with it. The Widow Brawnlyn had tried desperately to track the man down and kill him, lest he come back to oust her and take his rightful place. Only when the Giant paid Illyrica's ransom did she finally understand that her rival was living within her own borders, and when she grew bold enough, she tried to kill him by the hand of an incensed group of ignorant villagers. She failed—as has been recounted here. And the Giant showed her a coin from the treasure, nestled unmistakably in the palm of his hand, with its unspoken threat.

Genevieve knew all this. She suspected the truth: that the Giant had passed his title on to me, with the understanding that if the province ever needed rescuing, I was to rescue it. But while the land was under Genevieve, there was no need for me to leave my Castle for a civil throne.

I never knew why the Giant had done what he did: disappeared, taken up the life of a commoner, traded riches for a forest full of furs and a Castle full of innocents. Most puzzling to me was why he had never opposed the Widow when she so wickedly ruled over his people. Perhaps he did not know the truth of what she was—perhaps he felt that the people would not have him. Whatever the case, I have often looked over the legacy he left me and blessed him for making the choices he did. Though he denied his people rulership, what he gave to his adopted children was worth more than life. He gave them himself, and all of the love in his giant's heart.

For that, I will ever be grateful.

Rachel would love to hear from you!

You can visit her and interact online:
Web: **www.rachelstarrthomson.com**
Facebook: **www.facebook.com/RachelStarrThomsonWriter**
Twitter: **@writerstarr**

The Seventh World Trilogy

Worlds Unseen   Burning Light   Coming Day

For five hundred years the Seventh World has been ruled by a tyrannical empire—and the mysterious Order of the Spider that hides in its shadow. History and truth are deliberately buried, the beauty and treachery of the past remembered only by wandering Gypsies, persecuted scholars, and a few unusual seekers. But the past matters, as Maggie Sheffield soon finds out. It matters because its forces will soon return and claim lordship over her world, for good or evil.

The Seventh World Trilogy is an epic fantasy, beautiful, terrifying, pointing to the realities just beyond the world we see.

"An excellent read, solidly recommended for fantasy readers."
– Midwest Book Review

"A wonderfully realistic fantasy world. Recommended."
– Jill Williamson, Christy-Award-Winning
Author of *By Darkness Hid*

"Epic, beautiful, well-written fantasy that sings of Christian truth."
– Rael, reader

Available everywhere online or special order from your local bookstore.

The Oneness Cycle

  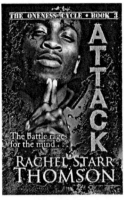

Exile   Hive   Attack

Coming Soon: Renegade and Rise

*The supernatural entity called the Oneness holds the world together.
What happens if it falls apart?*

When Tyler fishes the girl out of the bay, he thinks she's dead. She wishes she was. For Reese, life ended when the the Oneness threw her out. For Tyler, dredging Reese out of the water means life is nothing he thought. In a world where the Oneness exists, nothing looks the same. Dead men walk. Demons prowl the air. Old friends peel back their mundane masks and prove as supernatural as angels. But after centuries of battling demons and the corrupting powers of the world, the Oneness is under a new threat—its greatest threat. Because this time, the threat comes from within.

Fast-paced contemporary fantasy.

"Plot twists and lots of edge-of-your-seat action, I had a hard time putting it down! Waiting with great anticipation for the next in the series." —Alexis

"I sped through this short, fast-paced novel, pleased by the well-drawn characters and the surprising plot. Thomson has done a great job of portraying difficult emotional journeys . . . Read it!" —Phyllis Wheeler, The Christian Fantasy Review

Available everywhere online or special order from your local bookstore.

Novels by Rachel Starr Thomson

Available everywhere online or special order from your local bookstore!

Taerith

"Devastatingly beautiful" . . . *"Deeply satisfying."*

Lady Moon

"Laugh-out-loud funny"

"Reminiscent of Patricia C. Wrede and Terry Brooks's Magic Kingdom for Sale."

Reap the Whirlwind

"Haunting."

Theodore Pharris Saves the Universe

"Imaginative and hilarious."

Short Fiction by Rachel Starr Thomson

Available as downloads for Kindle, Kobo, Nook, iPad, and more!

Butterflies Dancing

Fallen Star

Of Men and Bones

Ogres Is

Journey

Magdalene

The City Came Creeping

Wayfarer's Dream

War With the Muse

Shields of the Earth

And more!

CPSIA information can be obtained
at www.ICGtesting.com
Printed in the USA
BVOW00s2132231216
471489BV00003B/141/P